A BEAUTIFUL YOUNG WOMAN

A BEAUTIFUL YOUNG WOMAN

A Novel

JULIÁN LÓPEZ

TRANSLATED FROM THE SPANISH BY
Samuel Rutter

Melville House
Brooklyn · London

A BEAUTIFUL YOUNG WOMAN

First published by Eterna Cadencia Editora

First Melville House printing: November 2017

Melville House Publishing
46 John Street
Brooklyn, NY 11201
and
8 Blackstock Mews
Islington
London N4 2BT

mhpbooks.com
facebook.com/mhpbooks
@melvillehouse

"Bien Pudiera Ser" by Alfonsina Storni, first published 1919, *Irremediablemente*, Buenos Aires Cooperativa Editorial Limitada

ISBN: 978-1-61219-681-7

Library of Congress Cataloging-in-Publication Data

Names: López, Julián, 1965- | Rutter, Samuel, translator.
Title: A beautiful young woman : a novel / Julian Lopez ; translated from the Spanish by Samuel Rutter.
Other titles: Muchacha muy bella. English
Description: First English language edition. | Brooklyn, NY : Melville House, 2017. | First published in Spanish as Una muchacha muy bella. Primera ediciâon. Buenos Aires : Eterna Cadencia, 2013.
Identifiers: LCCN 2017026694 (print) | LCCN 2017037971 (ebook) | ISBN 9781612196824 (reflow able) | ISBN 9781612196817 (paperback)
Subjects: LCSH: Children of disappeared persons--Argentina--Fiction. | Mothers and sons--Argentina--Fiction. | Political violence--Argentina--History--20th century--Fiction. | Abduction--Argentina--Fiction. | Loss (Psychology)--Fiction. | Psychological fiction. | BISAC: FICTION / Political. | FICTION / Historical. | GSAFD: Political fiction.
Classification: LCC PQ7798.422.O647 (ebook) | LCC PQ7798.422.O647 M8313 2017 (print) | DDC 863/.7--dc23
LC record available at https://lccn.loc.gov/2017026694

Designed by Betty Lew

Printed in the United States of America
1 3 5 7 9 10 8 6 4 2

For Francisco,

for Elsi,

for Delia,

for Oscar,

for Guillermo.

A BEAUTIFUL YOUNG WOMAN

My mother was a beautiful young woman. Her skin was pale and opaque; I could almost say it was bluish, and it had a luster that made it unique, of a natural aristocracy, removed from mundane trivialities. Her hair was black, of course—I already said she was a beautiful young woman—her hair was straight but heavy, and she wore it in a way that I haven't seen since. I'm not talking about her hairstyle: no matter what she did with it, her hair fell gracefully and in shape and always seemed tidily cut. I'm talking about the outline of her hair, of the linear sketch of that ocean of flexible antennae rushing into the sea of her face. Her hair began symmetrically and became visible in its contrast, each strand powerful, and it traced a subtle heart at the top of her head as it flowed down over her elegant temples.

My mother was a beautiful young woman, and she was voluptuously delicate; even as we spent our lives in almost total solitude, she had an extraordinarily sensual way of being, just for herself. Of course, I was there too, only seven years old, and she was like that just for me.

She spoke in a way that was profound but at the same time stripped of pretension, of appearing intellectual, or even seductive. In the middle of pronouncing an unusual word, she loved to linger in her own language. Verbal instincts kept her lively, and she would pull her heavy hair from one side to the other like the sumptuous cape of a bullfighter; she would lock her brown eyes on the ground—have I already said that my mother was a beautiful young woman?—and then slowly raise them to meet mine, starting again quickly with her lines of argument that were almost always indignant, almost always offensive, almost always naïve.

We lived in a two-room apartment with a bright kitchen that looked out into the light well of a modest but sophisticated building, one of those constructions from the 1950s with no more than three floors and no elevator, cool in summer and freezing once autumn arrives. Our home had a bathroom festooned with black mosaic tiles, pale green porcelain, and once-grand bathroom fixtures that had worn down faster than one turns the pages of a several-seasons-old fashion magazine. The apartment had a balcony that was unusable—merely opening the sliding door caused the moldings to crumble off in chunks. My mother hated the soot that came in from the avenue two blocks away, and she hated the noise that came from even farther away, from the auto shop and the truck beltway, and she was afraid of the birds that made their nests in the ash trees that shaded our two windows. One time I saw her in my bedroom hiding from a pigeon chick, still without its feathers, that the mother bird had thrown out of the nest because of its imperfections. It lay dying on the edge of our balcony. With a stick I pushed it over the edge so that my mother could come out of her hiding place and the tiny monster could end its gasping directly on the street below.

For a while, I kept an eye on the chick to try to see the exact moment the gelatinous mass would settle, the exact second of the final death rattle. It had no feathers, and its eyelids were still sealed, but it had been snubbed by its own mother and feared by mine; it deserved to die quickly.

The house was a living room with red walls that ran up to plastered ceilings hiding fluorescent tubes that tended to flicker in rhythmic agony rather than light up the room. A few adornments hung from the walls: a Mexican sombrero, made of silver, about the size of the palm of a small hand; a bronze casting of an Aztec sun with a sour expression and a colorful woven beard with a handful of bells on the end; a framed photograph of Anouk Aimée and Jean-Louis Trintignant that my uncle had sent from Paris; a photograph of Che Guevara, whom my mother called her boyfriend, stuck to the wall with a pin; a reproduction of a graffiti by Alonso—a woman sitting on the ground, her back arched and seemingly naked—and a few other postcards.

My mother liked postcards from Holland in tulip season; she bought them herself, wrote little travel tales on the backs of them, and put them in the post so that I would receive them about forty days later. Then we would get together in the kitchen to drink tea and eat fruitcake, and she would tell me everything she hadn't been able to write in the small space of the postcard. My mother loved describing all the tiny details of the journey: the red valleys where poppies grew spontaneously, the measured comforts of the carriage in the train that arrived from the Urals, skirting around the Danube or that took her first to Pest and then Buda, or the delicious violet sweets that were sold in the patisserie Sachel, in Vienna. My mother's dark pupils grew large with fascination, and she made the most of the storytelling, using it to instruct me on a range of matters, from the geography of daydreams to the anthropology of European exaggerations.

Up until that point, my mother had never left the country and had only visited Chapadmalal, the Río Tercero dam, Córdoba, Necochea, Tandil, La Reja, Highway 12, and El Etrusco, a little hotel in Paraná.

Nonetheless, every time she visited a new neighborhood, she returned home like Marco Polo exhausted by the excitement of his journey. She would tell me about the strange customs of our neighbors in Floresta or in Villa Real, the types of trees they had by their sidewalks, if she had seen packs of street dogs, if she had discovered libraries or museums, or if she had seen an old man urinating in a drain.

We loved to travel, and I took the opportunity to pick out the pieces of shiny fruit from the cake and peep through the holes they made while my mother, completely engrossed by her stories, gathered them up with surprising dexterity and ate them without noticing and without scolding me.

At nighttime the living room became a bedroom. That's where she slept, on a sofa that folded out and provided comfort after a laboriously complex set-up process. My mother complained that she could never find sheets that would fit her stretcher—they were either too long or too wide, and even small sheets weren't the right size for her bed. One time she came home with a shopping bag filled with a piece of white percale, a huge pair of silver-colored scissors, some needles, and a spool of thread. The first thing she did was get out her thimble, a porcelain treasure handed down from the diluted women of who knows which generation of the family on her father's side. A jewel that no one used, beautiful but uncomfortable, loaded with an unbearable power: the smudged history of those women who arrived to us *all mordant, defeated, and mutilated* through my grandfather's line.

I watched her face as she unfolded the handkerchief in which she kept the thimble, and I never knew what that word was, the one that I had to spell out from the air of the moment to comprehend the scene before me.

"Tomorrow, I'll make them," she said with enthusiasm.

The bag with the white percale transformed into a cat, and with each new day it became more and more comfortable between the cushions of the sofa until it became an unnoticed bundle. Each time night fell and the living room needed to be turned into a bedroom, I heard her rediscover the bundle and mew softly to herself, "Tomorrow . . ."

Then one day I stopped seeing the bag altogether, and the percale became a stuffed animal perched high up on a shelf.

Our house wasn't a good place for pets.

I remember seeing three books on the tiny table that only became her nightstand once her bed had been made and her hair rested on the pillow. There must have been many more, but I remember only these: *The Golden Bough*, a study of magic and religion by James Frazer, published by the Economic Culture Fund, *One Hundred Years of Solitude*, and *The Manipulated Man* by Esther Vilar. Of the one Latin American book, the title alone was enough to summon all my prejudice against the author; I wasn't going to allow myself to be drawn into all that. How much time had my mother spent carrying that book around, how many times had I seen her slip it into her purse before heading out, and how many times had she placed it back on the table, the very first thing she did when she got home? The blue squares and the red letters on the cover were a printed motif that stayed with us a long time— with us, a *long* time. Perhaps even for a whole century. I knew that book by heart.

I remember the impact that the end of the Vilar's dedication to the reader had upon me; I think it was the first time, and I'm not sure if it was the only time, that I heard a book as it spoke to me: "To those who are too old, too ugly, too sick . . ."

Of the other book, I remember only that it had many pages and that my desire to read dwindled very quickly after the first few lines. Reading always fascinated me, but books always ceased to be interesting almost at the same time as I took them on a plane and decided to venture forth into adventure. Books seem like women. Or they seem like men.

When we were at home my mother used to shell green beans, broad beans, or pods of black beans; I can't recall the meals she made with these vegetables, although I do recall the steam and the brilliance of some of them. Other vegetables perfectly resembled the skin of the long and elegant fingers on my mother's hand. Her index finger passed smoothly but firmly over the vegetable seams and found the exact spot where the structure would give way under pressure, an inaudible creaking that unsealed the natural lock of the beans and instantly made the green pearls or the veined buttons fall into the bowl, where they would bounce until finding their definitive resting place.

My mother was like the perfect murderer of vegetables;

I watched her do away with them with a natural coolness of which she herself was not truly aware.

Every now and again she stopped for a moment and lit a 43 70 cigarette, rotating through her tasks. But for her, in those moments, it didn't seem to me like a sensual pleasure. Perhaps due to smoking a mix of dark and blond tobacco, rather than affirming her with a "You've come a long way, baby," each puff seemed to paint her as a country girl who looked on in terror at the road signs, frightened in her flight, only a few steps beyond the limits of town.

I think I can remember (although, is it just a strip of loose images that I'm editing together to have a magnificent film, a story to tell myself?) that my mother's hands spent entire afternoons peeling vegetables and that in the evenings I had to empty the tea towels my mother deployed in the kitchen to catch the waste from the broad beans and the peas, the empty pods and the tangle of green fibers.

I put everything in plastic bags my mother made appear from one of the drawers in the larder as if to suggest I should free her from all the mess. I did it just as the sun went down, when my mother shut herself up in the tiny service room we had behind the laundry room, to cry—or to curse I suppose—or to plan the best lives in which I might not have appeared.

In truth, I don't think I ever filled one of those bags. What I'll never forget is the smell of the incinerator room. The black void when I lowered the hatch, the fresh air that flowed out of its dark mouth, the need to build up the courage to let go of the bag, not being able to run away quickly enough to avoid hearing the bag fall and bounce into the basement, because I had to close the hatch again before getting out as quickly as I could, spurred on by impalpable monsters. I don't know exactly why I walked toward the incinerator with an assuredness that I myself was not aware of, my feet flat on the ground, my footsteps firm, precise, and silent to avoid any blunder that might hold me back. I don't know why I was so assured; if I really paid attention, if I stayed behind to listen, that black mouth that led down to the basement could have spoken to me.

My mother was a beautiful young woman, and she loved me. But it's not difficult to suppose that there is quite a distance from being a beautiful young woman, in love with an incredibly handsome man who offered perpetual romance, to becoming an abandoned mother.

A distance that became the flesh and blood—and then "all eyes," as the ladies in the building used to say—that was me.

A human being who was nearly always silent and obedient—except when I shut myself in my bedroom during the times when my mother made herself scarce, to cry or to curse, or to plot the most effective ways to make me disappear.

My mother loved me. Even more than that, I could say my mother loved me madly. My mother loved me, of course; but I was her son.

That beautiful young woman listed my virtues while she stroked my hair. I suppose she was dictating out loud the list of abilities through which I could free her from the yoke of motherhood. As if with those caresses she was, in fact, feeding me, with a moral nourishment that swelled the muscles of a manhood that when the moment arrived, would relieve her, would make her proud, would make her forget the drabness with which her liberating dreams had been stained.

Whilst she rattled off these oaths, she sunk her fingernails with great gentleness into the trails that opened up in my hair and traced the outline of my head while reciting the rosary of my qualities. That's how we passed the hours of the afternoon.

Sometimes, and only very few times (but the problem is I can never forget them), her fingers stumbled over a double cowlick on the top of my head and tensed up. From the friction against my hair came an almost inaudible rustling, and then pearls began to fall from my mother's eyes and she gave in to an unhinged but self-controlled race to shut herself up in the service room.

I went and combed my hair in front of the bathroom mirror. I simply wet the comb with a little water, and I smoothed out the wild jungle my mother had left on top of my head.

Unlike her, I'm redheaded. My hair is a messy and endless amount of notes that remind her of my progenitor. A permanent wildfire, my mother used to say, and like terrified sheep, her desire to extinguish me escaped through her eyes.

My mother was a beautiful young woman. My mother loved me and knew intimately my potential virtues. My mother admired the seed of a man that was inside me.

But I was her son.

Once a month my mother dressed me in my little sky-blue outfit, a lightweight guayabera-style suit with little golden buttons and shorts that she had made for special occasions. She took me for lunch to the Bambi Patisserie or to the cinema and then afterward for tea at the Steinhauser Café or Casa Suiza. She said that every month we would have an outing "just like everyone else," although I have such fleeting memories that I doubt the monthly regularity was observed. I suppose that the happiness the plan promised and the desire to multiply the moments of pleasure with me made my mother believe it was an endurable ritual that could be repeated periodically. I could never be sure, but I don't know that we ever went to the same place more than once, although of course it was repeated in my memory, in the conversations when my mother told me how much fun we'd had in those extraordinary places she'd taken me.

I loved Bambi. It was a unique restaurant in Buenos Aires, on a tree-lined street in Barrio Norte, casual but distinguished, yet not too expensive. The curious thing about it was that you served your own food from trays upon which every item on the menu already sat. I always chose a little bottle of peach-flavored Delifrú, and my mother chose a tomato-flavored one seasoned with celery salt, the most delicious flavor of course, and the same one I would have chosen if it weren't for the fact that her choosing turned it into a modernism for adults only. Back then in the city there was no place like it, and so the outing became extravagant and sophisticated.

I loved Steinhauser; the strawberry tarts were a real event, luminous like stained-glass windows up high in the nave of a gothic cathedral and delicious as only the best German pastries can be. I enjoyed feeling elegant and sharing with my mother the pride of spending some time on a special outing that I would never be able to recount to my schoolmates, because the most charming thing about it was the symbolism of it all, and back then I couldn't quite comprehend it. Once I tried to tell Darío, who sat next to me, all about it. I tried to tell him what a tart was; I suppose my description made him see something like suspension bridges hanging in the fog because the look on his face became more and more concentrated as I tried to be more specific. At some point I stopped. My failure was so obvious that I stopped talking right in the middle of a sentence that, for my friend, seemed pretentious.

Like a big meringue, he'd said.

Of Casa Suiza, I remember that the first thing the waiter brought out was a silver triolet tray alongside a glass platter with little pastries arranged according to how moist they were and what they had inside them. I'll never forget my disappointment when I found out that they're "not for eating." I thought they were a part of our tea, which we used to take with toasted sandwiches of ham, cheese, and tomato, but the first time that bounty of cream and marzipan and almonds and tiny little brioches sprinkled lightly with sugar like snow was laid before me I didn't hesitate to dig in.

My mother intercepted my swiping hand, and I'm not sure how, with what strong words, or with what action, but she informed me of the tragedy. The pastries were a devil's bargain; they weren't included in the price of tea, and it was a habit of the patisseries to tempt their diners with delights that would that would swell the final bill each time a greedy hand made them disappear one by one from the tray.

For me this was an incomprehensible cruelty; it filled me with disbelief that we could keep on living in the face of such a thing, as if we were walking along a path in the fresh air, in a Versailles-esque picnic, never realizing we were stepping barefoot on a nest of venomous snakes in the slums of New Delhi. I couldn't comprehend it, and I looked over at the tables where the triolet tray was visited with permission: tables peopled by large and ostentatious women who seemed to delight in the selection of the most promising pastries, the ones with most cream, the ones that were most delicious.

My mother always drank strong coffee—a double. After the first sip she would light a cigarette, take a long drag, and then forget about it in the ashtray. It wasn't unusual for her to repeat this action and find herself smoking two cigarettes at once. I suppose she liked the sensation of the new, the inaugural, and that when the matter began to repeat itself her memory disappeared.

She was crazy about ice cream sodas, she loved them. She would tell me with her eyes ablaze about the long tricolor glasses of her childhood, the unforgettable afternoons in La Vascongada with her cousins, her siblings, and the tubular vessel in which the ruby of the grenadine, the smoothness of the cream, and the explosion of the soda bubbles slowly mixed together. It was wonderful to hear her speak so passionately, to know that she was so easily pleased by those treats and the sharing of a simple childhood, surrounded by equals.

In Casa Suiza, or in whichever café we visited, she would call over the waiter with great refinement, and then with a cheeky and smiling urgency she ordered her double espresso, an ashtray, and "a large vanilla ice cream soda for my son."

I never really liked ice cream with soda, cream, and grenadine, and I imagined I'd like a different treat more. I was dying to sit at a café on a corner in Buenos Aires and look out a window, read a newspaper, and drink endless cups of double espresso, smoke my pack of 43 70s until I filled every ashtray in the place with butts. But I decided to make her happy—which, in this case, seemed so easy to do—and I smiled at the ice cream soda full of sugar and the colored syrup that made me nauseous.

Because I only took a few sips just to please her, at the end of our afternoon tea, my mother's mood darkened a little. "Why do people order things if they don't want to eat them?" she would say. "It's a waste, an ice cream soda sitting there like that. The movies, a patisserie, everything under the sun," she would pronounce, crushing her cigarette against the ashtray and calling the waiter again to ask for the check—refined but curt this time. Then she would pay and get up with deliberate movements.

Who spoke for my mother, and to whom? Who were those "people" who appeared and put an end to our outing? Who spoke inside my mother?

There is a dark light—I could almost say it was bluish—a light that defines the perimeters of the world in such a way as I have never seen in another room, as if certain leaves refract an opacity that shimmers and translates luminosity in a more material manner, a more granular manner. Something happens in the air of those rooms; everything seems calm. And everything seems both strange and recognizable.

My mother often took me to the botanical gardens. We spent long afternoons in the silence imposed by those rapturous gardens. It was incredible to be in the middle of the city and then suddenly come across such verdure amid all the rough and muted blue; every sound was magnified, each footstep was a reminder that we walked there on our own feet, and each footstep supposed an act of unknowing consequences. A trail of dying insects behind us, of freshly shooting buds, of fungal spores pressed down inside their reproductive copula, everything lived there in the splendor attracted by the moisture in the granules of air, in those immaterial pools that multiplied the system.

Every single one of our footsteps had consequences; they reminded us that we were there, a mother and her son passing through the forest. An amniotic space amid urban electricity, paths of luminous darkness, and Victorian silence.

There was a whole world there for me, a place full of mystery and beauty. But the only thing I could do was contemplate it, enter into an enforced trance, visit the carp in their tanks and dream that I stroked their flanks while they gifted back to me their nobility and fidelity, just like the animals in *Blancos caballos de agosto*.

The natural world was an unsettling experience. We went down those cool and opaque tunnels, and then suddenly we emerged into round clearings where the sun shone on beautiful rocks. The neatness of the light and shadow was astonishing. They were perfectly delineated kingdoms, although their lineage was mixed along some branches. The green leaves that irradiated blue seemed like secret sentinels. In any case, this was clear: every single thing and every single one of the states of that place was a voice that proffered silence. We walked through the tunnels, and suddenly we caught sight of terraces of light at the end, and we went out into them.

My mother's eyes filled with tears at the sight of every sculpture: *The First Chills*, an old bearded man sitting down and embracing a girl; *Sagunto*, a mother who sacrifices her son and then takes her own life to escape Hannibal's advancing army; the series of sculptures dedicated to Beethoven's Sixth Symphony; *Flora Argentina*. Almost all of them were reproductions of European originals.

We stopped in front of each work, and she would read out the information about the sculptors (I only remember hearing men's names), the characteristics of the piece, and their stories from the plaques. In her voice, these stories became a sort of exaggeratedly somber master class, although I was fascinated to know the names of those who had been able to shape the earth's rocks. It fascinated me just as much as standing before *Saturnalia* or *Columna Meteorológica*, a gift from the Austro-Hungarian community for the centenary of the Republic, in gratitude for having welcomed the wave of citizens from its crumbling empire.

I became aroused among so many Venuses. I walked up, in the same measured footsteps used by lovers who enter a chapel to marry, walked around them slowly, as if my eyes could caress them in a completely new way. I circled around them and discovered that they were alive. I scrutinized them like a serious child so that they would reveal to me the secrets they clearly possessed. Or I made as if to set upon them, to catch them trembling or gasping so they would have to give themselves over to me, for the mistake of revealing themselves. I spoke to them in the language of the devoted, a mental language that few children know and that I believed turned me into a steady enchanter of silent ways. I had an unbridled desire for them to catch sight of me from their stone and rest their gaze upon me.

I wanted them to choose me over their own eternal beauty. I wanted them to look at me and return to life.

My mother used to leave me on my own for a while, sitting on the wooden slats of one of the wrought iron benches, near the little waterfall of the artificial stream that appeared and disappeared from view according to the bends of the path. Back then it was normal for children to be left alone a while in a public place. Kidnappings were highly unlikely—they were almost unimaginable, unknown. At a certain moment, my mother would begin to grow anxious and lose patience with me. She changed her battery of gestures, and although this was imperceptible from her appearance, I knew that this would signify the moment of solitude. One of the passwords that unlocked the moment was unmistakable: she would mumble a string of half-pronounced words that ended with the clear diction of "Always hiding behind his mother's skirts." She didn't say it to me, at least not directly, although it was obvious that my only occupation was (is?) being with her. Who could be talking to my mother, who could accuse her of being a coward? She never looked at me when she said it, and she wasn't addressing her words to me. But there I was. There I was, hiding behind her skirts.

One time we came across a lady with her children, a girl and a boy; the boy was calm, sitting on one of those wrought iron benches, although he seemed absorbed in an activity that excluded others, you could almost hear the humming of a tiny engine between his eyes on his slightly malevolent face. I remember that I found the scene attractive; it was the image of a sort of evil genius in the midst of scheming. How extraordinary to catch someone in that moment before! At the stage in which everything is still perfect in its potential.

To one side, on a terrace made of gravel from crushed bricks, the girl played alone. She spoke the different voices of each of her characters as they responded to one another and displayed a stupidly harmonious community in the lightness of her little body. She was a girl determined to show everyone that she was convinced of her girlhood, covered in terracotta dust.

My mother approached the woman and struck up a casual conversation, the woman told her about her children, about how nice it was to enjoy these days of sunshine in the botanical gardens. In an instant it was clear that with just a few sentences—and with the skill of an assassin of vegetables—she had arranged for me to stay there with them, under the protective gaze of the woman who sat knitting beneath a willow, while my mother slipped away for a few minutes. My mother's maneuvering was a strategy to avoid even the most minimal gesture of reprobation from the other lady. With regard to me, she knew I was aware that naturally, a woman, sooner or later, has to slip away.

She looked at me and said, "Why don't you play with that little boy?" She looked at him and said, "What's your name, sweetie?"

"Santi," replied the boy, who seemed to be an expert in conceding answers to questions that if they were posed in open conflict, he would clearly lose in advance. "Santi," he said, as if explaining to my mother that he was answering her only to save himself from the slap across the face he would surely receive from his mother if he dared to give a more honest answer of "What's it to you?"

After retrieving this password for me, my mother left quickly, following the snaking path of the water far beyond the waterfall.

A slave to her secret service tactics, I sat down next to Santi, but I made no attempt at contact. He was a child, but he looked like an old man, dressed in a handmade woolen sweater, from a pattern that would fit a middle-aged man, an old lady in a retirement home, or a little girl more or less living on the streets. He was sitting with an exaggerated tranquility, as if he were focusing on breathing.

I don't know how long we sat there like that, swinging our feet in our round-toed, lace-up shoes, mine brown, his black, without speaking a word to each other.

"Santi," he said directly to me in an almost conspiratorial tone and as if he were inviting me to join in a conversation with colleagues during the five minutes it takes to smoke a cigarette, far from the bosses. God knows all I wanted to do was tell him my name straightaway and break into a lively and animated conversation about our interests. I was prepared to think nothing of what he would say to me, to not jump to conclusions or draw mental sketches of his opinions, which—after all, he was only a boy—would surely seem banal to me.

The devil knows all I wanted to do was tell him my name. But I expected so much from myself that the letters piled up on my tongue and my mouth opened by itself. "Santi," I said.

I lowered my gaze and returned to the soles of our shoes swinging in the air beneath the slats of the wooden bench.

Santi didn't appear to notice my disappointment, and I suppose he assumed that we shared the same name and this excited him. At one point he moved forward in complete slowness and said, "Watch this."

My eyes followed him obediently, and he smiled to the side, a tiny smirk leaving me in no doubt that he would make me his accomplice. Santi ducked down and picked up one of the little rocks of crushed brick, making sure none of his movements were noticed by his mother, who was knitting together a tangle of horrible colors and moving her thin lips along with every thrust of her needles.

Santi marked his forehead with the little orange rock and let out a muffled but audible "ay," a wounded cry that masked something serious. Then he dropped the rock and raised his hands to his forehead while contorting his face in mute pain. The sequence of events was so rapid, it left me astounded. I couldn't understand what happened to him or why he asked me to watch. In response to his noise, his mother lifted her gaze and showed her sharp features.

"Can't you breathe? Is that it, what's wrong, son?" she said in a voice that couldn't be anything other than a mother's voice, or a principal's voice, or a nurse's voice at a sanitary checkpoint on the border, or the voice of someone deaf from birth. The combination of wool that the lady was knitting together was nothing short of insulting, and I wondered which of these children's bodies would have to wear such an ensemble. But the palette of wool wasn't the only horrible thing, the entire lady herself was a problem of proportional perception. *How could my mother have chosen her if it weren't one of her tricks that made her look like a normal person engaged in normal activities?* I thought, without being able to articulate it completely.

"What happened my son? What is it? Tell Mama," said the lady, as if in that moment the world needed any more vulgarity.

Parsimoniously and with his head barely tilted, Santi slowly uncovered his forehead with the orange mark ringed with red from the pressure of his fingers. Without changing the position of his head even by a millimeter and rolling his eyes back as far as they could go he began to speak. "It was Yani," he said. "From over there she saw me sitting here with my little friend, Santi, and she picked up a stone and threw it at me, Mama."

Then he placed one of his hands back on his forehead, straightened his back a little, twisted himself around slightly, and looked at his sister, who continued playing her own little game without noticing anything.

I couldn't believe what I was hearing, and the excitement of it all seriously threatened the health of my heart. Where had this malevolent little man come from, so unscrupulous and sure of his efficacy?

The lady stood up, stuck the needles into her ball of yarn, put it into her string bag, and left it all on the bench. As parsimonious as her son, she began to walk directly toward the little girl, who, once she noticed the huge body of her mother arriving, raised a smiling face and then squinted her eyes because the sun struck her full in the face.

It was the perfect movement for her mother's slap to be laid upon her face like an outlandish ruby, for it to sound out clearly and to make the girl roll across the little piles of crushed brick that she had arranged for her game. "You're the skin of Judas! Bad girl!" her mother screamed. "Are you trying to tell me that it annoys you to see your brother sitting over there with his little friend Santi?"

Before the scene of the little girl knocked over in the orange dust, the woman had a slight hesitation, a millisecond of doubt, I suppose that the sonorous slap took her by surprise also, but then, recomposed, she added, "And get up from there and dust off your dress—it's in tatters from all that rolling around on the ground!" After the spite of her final word she turned around, walked back to her seat, and took out her knitting from that awful bag.

Santi sighed and seemed relieved, looser, more childlike. He grinned at me and told me that woolen pants made him itch, that the itching made him nervous, and that he thought that the scientists should invent a smooth and light fabric that didn't cause eczema. *Silk*, I thought a bit haughtily, but I was unable to speak because I was still taken by surprise.

"Do you want me to show you?" he asked with a jolt, and before I could answer he began to pull down his pants and his underwear on one side until a raised, purplish streak appeared on the whitest part of his flesh near his groin. With an enthusiastic look on his face, he said, "I also have it on my neck and behind my knees and on my elbows, and sometimes I get it on my face."

Now Santi was breathing more comfortably. His mother's voice made us look up: "Never forget that other kids have that inside of them, my son. They have it in their hearts," she said, and she smiled at him with a face that made me sad.

His sister had picked herself up in complete silence and had begun to brush off the red dust with complete gentleness. The rays of sunshine that separated her from us were filled with tiny microscopic pebbles, and they seemed like shining prison bars that left her stranded on the other side from us. "Get out of here, dummy!" yelled the mother. "Go and brush yourself off behind the greenhouse, will you? You're going to irritate your brother's chest."

Then she looked at me and said, "Santi's asthmatic, you see? He's not allowed to do anything."

All of a sudden everything seemed to grow silent, and I'm not sure why, but we both looked up at the footpath that led off in front of us. As if the air itself had rippled to announce the arrival of an apparition, we began to see, at the end of the path, a beautiful young woman. My mother had come back to rescue me from a scene that didn't quite enchant or horrify me, but perhaps did both of those things and more: it captivated me completely, like those shining fish that stop moving in terror at the sight of the fierce cuttlefish that hunts them.

My mother wasn't asthmatic, but she too seemed relieved upon her return, although when she arrived I realized that I didn't know the exact word to define her way of returning. It wasn't quite relief exactly; it was a changing mix of things, a renewed charge, a better architecture for the weight she carried.

Every time she came back, it seemed to me like she had something different, but I could never identify what it was, if her clothing was slightly askew, or her hair looser, or if all that had changed was that her face had relaxed a little. Perhaps my mother was more of a woman when she came back.

She walked in a way that was delicate, voluptuous, and elegant; she had smooth black hair, and it always looked recently trimmed in a style I had never seen before.

Seeing her arrive was like a party that, for some reason, I always avoided celebrating. A party that made me a little sad. My mother was a dark-haired woman, with pale, opaque skin—I'd almost say it was bluish—and she wore tweed skirts lined with silk.

My mother was a beautiful young woman.

She loved to say that her skirts were made of tweed, like the skirts worn by female characters in detective novels. Although her skirts were never made of tweed or lined with silk, my mother was an elegant woman. A very beautiful young woman.

I didn't know why, but every time I saw my mother coming back from one of her escapades that made her look like that, even though they might have been brief departures, it made me not want to be her son. All I wanted was to escape from there, to be big and grown, to greet her with admiration and say to her in a firm voice, "You've come a long way, baby."

Santi and I were seated together on the same bench, our dark swaying diminished the impulse of our last swing, the image of my mother on the path seemed to make the leaves fall slower and more gracefully from the trees, spirals that came down through the air as if to land at the bottom of a pool.

That Santi also kept his feet still was a confirmation I needed: it was clear, a beautiful young woman was approaching from that direction. I saw his enraptured face, and then that boy sitting next to me on the bench looked back at me with an expression that ended up making me sad. I suppose it must have been a congenital condition, something suffered by everyone in his family. On their faces, a smile looked like a grimace, a little buoy lost in a sea of sadness.

Santi looked back at the path, and that woman, just a few steps away from us, was once again my mother. Things went back to their normal state, and the autumn settled the mutability in the air, the speed and the trajectory of the racing leaves of the oaks, the poplars, and the acacia trees.

"How did he behave himself?" my mother asked as she watched Santi's mother stick her knitting needles into her ball of yarn, understanding nothing. I looked at him again: Santi was swinging his feet, his hands clenched into fists resting on the bench and his shoulders hunched all the way up to his neck, then he was calm again, like the deep end of a pool, where a boy would drown if he fell in.

The girl came back from the greenhouse with only a very few traces of orange dust on her dress but with her ponytail a little messy, and she stood next to her own mother, watching my mother, who dominated the scene with movements that seemed like ballet in this context. The girl was a little less of a girl now, and the simple imaginary community that had once kept her company had been disbanded and had left her alone; it made her feel like shouting at those bodies in exile that moved off into the distance, walking backward: "Hey! Come back! You forgot me, the girl!"

It seemed to me that we were all sad because it was easier than being angry. But where did I get these ideas from, and at what moment did the fierce aquamarine of that scene turn into the dying light of a cloudy afternoon over a river that lies about its meekness, to become the night?

Santi's mama had put away her knitting and stood up next to my mother in a ceremony that showcased their bodies like unequivocal postcards for maternity. To one side, the girl, sitting on the bench, rooted around in her mother's purse and took out a bottle of perfume that she shook before opening.

She daubed her index finger with it, then painted herself with fragrance behind the ears. Attracted by the movement and in full possession of a new character, my mother said, "What looooovely perfuuuume, my deeeear."

The girl regained a little of her childhood and answered her like a girl once again. "It's *swee honestí,* madame," she said, making her best attempt at the English label, before her mother corrected her: Sweet Honesty, from Avon, a label that seemed like an extraordinary and unjust settling of scores. For the first time that afternoon, I gave my respects to the lady. For the first time that afternoon, Santi's mother displayed her weapons to a battle that I have no idea why my mother initiated.

My mother said, "Well, off we go," and I got up from the bench thinking, *Off we go, just the two of us, off we go.*

I stood up very slowly in honor of Santi, who was watching his shoes swinging and looking at them as if they were boats that dragged his feet to and fro uncontrollably. He was serious, and you could almost hear the humming of a little motor of concentration deep inside that made him frown.

I began to walk while I took in the scene of the mothers: disdain from mine and a pantomime of distraction from Santi's. To one side, his sister began to enter again into her imaginary community, and now it was my new and fleeting and surprising friend who was left alone.

When I stood next to my mother, the smell was truly overwhelming. If honesty was such a sweet treat that it invited me to retch, then perhaps I could understand the things that I did not understand: my mother's tones of voice and her airs of a chaste diva.

When I stood next to my mother, I put my right hand in the left-hand pocket of her coat, and the coolness of the silk returned something to me that I didn't even know I had almost lost: the feeling of softness and lukewarm coolness.

My mother thanked Santi's mother and began to walk, pulling me along from inside her pocket. "Wait a minute," said Santi's mother, and she picked up her bag and pulled out the bottle of perfume, shook it, opened it, and sprayed a little into the hollow of her left hand, then asked the little girl to close it, before rubbing her hands together and approaching me with a smile. Staring at me straight in the eyes she stroked my face and hair with hands damp with Sweet Honesty, then looked at my mother and said, "There you go, all primped and perfumed." It was a brutal caress.

"Say goodbye to your little friend Santi, Santi," she said, closing the scene, and my mother took my hand out of her pocket and walked off with me behind her, confused and aromatic, in a scene in which no one was a minor character.

I turned around and waved at Santi, who didn't see me, his neck hunched into his shoulders, as silent as a ship on a foggy night. Next to him a rosebush would have looked more lively.

My mother advanced through jasmine bushes from Paraguay, laurels, the dark bark of hardwood trees from Tucumán, and she immersed herself into the blue of one of the paths that would lead us to the exit.

Once we arrived at the sidewalk, the air seemed different and the light began to wane, the cats from the botanical gardens began to parade out from their dens. Following an afternoon of siestas, this bright but narcotic animality seemed like blotches from the night that was drawing near. Between the bars that marked the boundaries of the gardens, the cats began hatching the plots of their nocturnal escapades. They could see in the dark, but I wanted to get home before the dark.

For some reason my mother took me by the hand with a different firmness, and we walked in silence to the bus stop. My mother said nothing.

The whole street was silent: cars rumbled and their drivers shouted, but everything was silent.

"What are they throwing up against the wall?"

"What?" replied my mother.

"That," I said, pointing to some workers up high on a scaffold in a construction site.

"That's the cement they put over the bricks, so the walls are smooth. But you should ask Uncle Rodolfo about these things. He knows better."

"Yes, but he hasn't come around for a while."

"You know he's very busy, but one of these days he'll slip away for a quick visit. We should call him."

"Mama, are the workers poor? Are Santi and his mama and his sister poor?"

The afternoon light faded away gradually, my mother hurried along, and I kept walking without taking my eyes off the scaffold with those men so high up.

I was caught in her wake on the sidewalk. My legs couldn't keep up with my mother's large stride, and every now and again I tripped over myself and fell. The good thing was that I never managed to hurt myself; my mother pulled on me forcefully, and for a few seconds my legs kicked in the air as I tried to figure out the best way to return them to solid ground and begin walking again in a more efficient manner. If my slowness hadn't bothered my mother so much—the fury gritted between her teeth almost escaping her silent lips—I suppose I would have enjoyed that tumble through the air, and I would have imagined that after my pirouette, it was the turn of the elephants and the young trapeze artist. A diminutive and pretty young girl, in a sequined bodysuit, always on the edge of the abyss. She was set free during her aerial tricks, held up by the angst of those holding the net below, biting the clasp that made her spin like a whirlwind in the void and left her balanced on a knife edge of danger and imminence. Then, from an unlighted dome came a young man with strong thighs, raised buttocks, hands strong on the swing, and then again the heavenly breast of the young maiden of the air. All illuminated. She lay back and abandoned her responsibility to the flying man who sketched his won challenge in the air and obeyed, dutifully, the circus, and everything that was expected of him.

A bumpy gray screen swings across my eyes, covering my field of vision, and then suddenly the scene opens again, and they appear behind it, the trapeze artists, on the sand, hand in hand, smiling to the public. Another bumpy and gray screen coils from the beginning of the tail to the trunk of the next elephant that follows it, and then, once again, it's them, raising their free hands to signal the end of their performance, the grace with which they cloak themselves on the ground the same as in the air. Another gray tail links to another trunk, and that black and glassy eye, so slow in its gait with scant eyelashes, like a dark hollow, vaster than the highest rigging of the tent, with no little woman, no man, and no safety net.

There is only that vast eye that I lean toward, a predictable future of questions I will never be able to formulate to anyone. In that swinging I am stranded, my own childhood image reflected on the edge of a trapeze no one can see and that moves by the grace of a wind that never ceases and hovers by an unexpected mountain that approaches steadily.

"Can I change my name to Santi?" The words escape my mouth, climbing on the bus via the running board, while the driver gives the tickets to my mother and winks at her. She leans in and whispers, "Seems like he wants his own nom de guerre too."

And then a moment of confusion because of the people who don't have a ticket yet and want to board the bus that is already overfull, and the pale face of the driver after her comment, and my mother once again annoyed, grabbing me by the hand and pushing me in among the people standing, and my face squashed against coats, against purses, and excuse me, excuse me, and a man who stands up and gives us his seat, a real gentleman, and my name on tenterhooks because I haven't received a response, and the conceded seat, and my mother's skirt, and the whole window just for me.

"When we get home you're taking a bath. That way we'll get rid of that horrible smell, what a revolting perfume! Plenty of soap on your face, please. Use some of Mama's shampoo in your hair, and put in some *savia* ointment too, because it has a strong smell, and leave it in for a while, or better still, don't wet your hair while I'm on the phone at Elvira's place."

When we arrived home my mother filled the bathtub halfway and left me a towel on the toilet lid, then she came into my room and said, "It's ready, get in the bath, I'm going over to Elvira's."

I had taken off all my clothes except for my socks and underwear, and I was circling my bedroom looking for some kind of ruse to avoid the soaking. I only managed that once and it took me so much effort that, in the end, I might as well have taken the bath. My mother's tone of voice removed all hope of avoiding it, and when she left my room, I went straight to the bathroom, took off my socks and underwear, and got in the bath. I stood there motionless because the water was scalding hot and my feet, ankles, and shins had turned red. My mother went out of the apartment and then came back in, entering the bathroom to give me a kiss. What a stink!

"Wash yourself, dry yourself properly, and then wrap yourself up in the bathrobe. I'll be back in a moment."

When I was alone again, I turned on the cold water faucet, which was the only thing that interested me about a bath: the gushing sound of cascades of water against water, a deep sound that I loved to listen to from beneath the surface as well. I waited a moment for the water to cool, and then I sat down and began to slip underneath the water with my eyes closed and my nose pinched. Once I was fully under I opened my eyes and I stayed down there as long as I could hold on, among those waves that sounded like submarines.

I couldn't stay long in one reverie, because as soon as one thing appeared, my imagination exploded and opened up like a Russian doll that made each scene smaller, more specific. The submarine didn't take long to become a shipwreck in the depths of a dark ocean, and the bathtub opened up like a sluice gate to the sea and attracted the most bloodthirsty sharks.

Almost leaping, I stood up again and lathered my body, I put shampoo in my hair, and I began to rinse off with the water that would stay in my cupped hands. My strategy to avoid submerging myself again was a total failure so I took a deep breath and sat down, slipping away again and sinking my head underneath to make all the foam on my hair disappear.

Elvira was our neighbor, a kind and old-fashioned lady who was one of the few people with a telephone in her apartment, and she let us use it. My mother said she had once been a tango singer, and it wasn't unusual to hear her singing sometimes, in a voice that, to me, sounded like it came straight out of the old movies, waltzes and milongas that seemed to be from another time and another country, just like her name, her hair, her smell, and the decorations in her apartment. My mother said that Elvira's house was a palace of crochet and *plumetí*, a type of Swiss cotton tulle with velvet buttons that covered the lampshades in her living room and bedroom. Everything was always very neat, and it was difficult to imagine that anyone could sit comfortably in those chairs that creaked and shone from the clear plastic covering, and the woolen socks on the chair legs to stop them marking the waxed parquet floor, and the handle of the kettle and the ice box wrapped up in little coats that she had knitted herself.

Elvira adored me, and every time she saw me, she asked me to flutter my eyelids. She said I had the prettiest eyelashes in the whole neighborhood, and she was enchanted to see them batting just for her, just because she asked.

She kissed my cheeks and told me she was crazy about me, that I was the love of her life. I let her do it even though her kisses were gross. I let her do it because she was good to us, because she was alone and lived with a little old dog called Ñata, a photo of her father, and an image of St. Anthony and the Virgin of Luján that Elvira said changed color with the weather, although I never saw it. I let her do it because when I stayed in her house, when my mother went away, Elvira would serve me a tiny cup of peppermint liqueur. It was our little secret—she would have several while I moistened my own lips several times from my cup, and the two of us picked at radishes preserved in oil and salt that she served from a little jar.

Some afternoons she would ring our doorbell and come over bearing a tray with a cake made of apples and raisins and walnuts covered with an immaculate napkin. She would leave it with my mother and say, "All I need back is the tray and the napkin." Then my mother would invite her to stay; it was just what Elvira was hoping for, and my mother would say to her, "Why don't you come in and give the man of the house a kiss?"

I liked Elvira—she was the only one in the building we interacted with. My mother avoided contact with the others and became very short if someone came up to her. One afternoon when she was taking me to the doctor, we came across a boy from the floor below who was playing in the street with his friends from the block. My mother and I would dress elegantly to go out, me in my little blue outfit with the brown coat and golden buttons, her in one of her characteristic tweed skirts with silk lining.

For these outings she would comb my hair with Brylcreem and dress me in socks that never fell down. When the neighbor saw us pass, he stopped playing and followed me with his gaze and asked, "Where are you going?"

"We're going to the movies," my mother butted in.

"Will you take me too, miss?"

"Sorry, dear, we're in a bit of a rush. Next time."

All this without us breaking stride. All while we were on our way.

Once we had turned the corner my mother said, "It's very vulgar to ask people where they're going—it's bad manners. I don't like it."

When I got out of the bath, I sat on the edge and began to dry myself with the towel, and I sniffed myself like a bloodhound to seek any trace of that Sweet Honesty that my mother and I both hated. There were now so many odors in the steam from the bath that I couldn't tell. I think I liked all of them.

I wanted to stay dripping, cover myself with the bathrobe, and lounge on the sofa watching TV, but my mother complained that I left her bed all wet. When I finished drying myself, I stood in front of the mirror to comb my hair to the side. I opened the cabinet to take out the black comb, and I saw the shaving brush that had been kept there forever. When I asked my mother who it belonged to, she usually said it was my grandfather's, but other times she mumbled a little—once she said it belonged to my uncle. I almost never had the courage to touch it, but that night I did. I took it out very carefully and put the bristles close to my nose to smell them, to breathe them in, to inhale any particle of a grown man that might linger there, in the history of shaving before me, from the unknown hand of the man who took the brush and covered his face with foam.

That was all that remained of this, in my house, and there had to be some reason why it remained there. Perhaps my mother too would breathe it in, or maybe she dared to brush her face with its softness that prickled like a beard.

. . .

Combed and wearing the bathrobe, I went to the sofa and turned on the television. Lili gathered her suitcase, walked along a painted path in the background, and then walked up the steps that led to the most dangerous trapeze and promised her a way out of her destiny as an orphan. The screen was gray but suddenly it seemed filled with color as Reynardo, Zsa Zsa the ballerina, and Carrot Top beckoned her over to settle their dispute about the puppets. I suppose that Mel Ferrer, hidden in the darkness of his little theater, felt like one of those men who was too old, too ugly, too sick, because he had a limp from World War II, and throughout the whole film he had a look on his face that made me sad.

I wanted to tell him that my mother had a book that was dedicated to him; I strained myself wondering how I could let him know so that he could stop waiting for whatever it was he was waiting for. I worked to convince myself, and every now and again I repeated this equation as if it were a lesson in logic, that whatever seemed sad at the beginning necessarily *had* to turn out happy in the end.

Zsa Zsa's beautiful puppet legs passed in front of Lili's fascinated eyes, and then the chords of that song started up that says that a song of love is a sad song and don't ask me how I know and I sit at the window and watch the rain and hi Lili hi Lili hi lo.

Toward the end, the camera enters the little theater and almost crashes into the man who brings the puppets to life. I got up quickly and ran once again to the mirror in the bathroom to look at my face. I wanted to see if I looked like Mel Ferrer, if I had that same look. What I saw was a twinge of preoccupation on a serious face. I looked at myself for a while; it was impossible to know what face I had if I interrogated an expression too long. I had to be super quick, as quick as Speed Racer. I practiced a few more times, but there was no way to shake off the expression of someone who is trying to capture an expression.

I went back to the sofa, and Lili already had another gaze upon her—now it was Mel Ferrer who wanted to capture her expression.

I'm not sure at what point I fell asleep, but my mother woke me up telling me that she had to rush out, that Elvira would come to stay with me, that she would make me bow tie pasta with butter, and that we could watch TV. So many concessions! Bow tie pasta with butter was my favorite food, far better than *milanesa* with mashed potatoes, and being able to watch TV at night pleased me to no end.

My mother went to the bathroom, tied her hair back in a ponytail, and washed her face with cold water. I watched her from the doorway, and then Elvira arrived shrieking about the love of her life. "Here I am," I said, while in the background the final music from *Lili* could be heard, and my mother came out of the bathroom without saying a word. She put on her coat, and, with a worried expression on her face, told me not to wait for her.

How could I not wait for you, I wanted to ask her, but Elvira had enveloped me in her web of kisses, and my mother took the opportunity to leave, almost running out the door. She added, "Don't wait *up* for me. Don't wait *up*."

From inside her robe Elvira revealed the neck of the bottle of peppermint liqueur, and while she gave me a wink, she opened one of her pockets, a nest from which two little resting doves were about to take flight: the little cups with handles in which she poured her own little version of absinthe. The tone of the evening had changed radically, and it seemed wonderful to be able to drink until I was good and drunk with a real dame by my side, even if this dame wore a quilted pink dressing gown, the collar and sleeves festooned with Swiss cotton tulle, a material that produced sparks if you rubbed it together, and wore slippers with terry cloth socks, her face greasy with ointments, her eyebrows gone and mustache appearing, and her head a tangle of rollers covered by a bonnet meant to look like silk.

"Where did Mama go?" I asked her.

"Ay, be quiet! *Pobre diabla* is starting!" she said, and twisted the knob on the television. A single point of light concentrated in the center, and suddenly a big bang made the entire universe appear on the screen. Solita pulled down on her tiny skirt and ran, all skinny and beautiful, across the sleepers of a railway track with a desperation that fixed my eyes to that image and made me breathe like a diver who reappears on the surface after holding out in the depths. The camera tracked this sexy little woman, who ran like a deer that had been startled by a furtive gunshot or a heavy presence or a twig that snapped underfoot.

The camera stayed with her, then suddenly zoomed out and showed a vast expanse of railway tracks, an area filled with silver rails and wooden sleepers where trains transported masses of people. It was the logic of worlds merging under the sign of work, a horrifying copulation of the city with the suburbs.

"How wonderful, how wonderful!" exclaimed Elvira, completely disentangled from me and given over to her native Guarani passion: she was like a songbird, trilling her bewitching harps from on high as soon as Arnaldo appeared on screen, with his sweet expression and his lips overripe as if he had just eaten every orange on the mountain.

"Why is it called *Pobre diabla*? Did you ever get married? Why is the show called *Pobre diabla*?"

Elvira was a statue frozen by the cathodically charged gorgon in the living room, and my charms as the love of her life had no power whatsoever. The show was, of course, much more interesting than me. Just like when my mother read *One Hundred Years of Solitude*, reclining on the sofa and completely engrossed in a way that drew me in but left me completely on the outside.

Elvira came back to life with the first commercials, poured herself a cup of peppermint liqueur, drank it down in one gulp, and filled the cup again. Only then did she notice me, filling my cup halfway and winking.

"I don't know why they called it *Pobre diabla*," she said without looking at me. "And I have my Ñata, my records, my show, my aunts in Tolosa . . ." She went silent, then buttoned up the highest part of her dressing gown, which had come undone with all the movements from pouring the liqueur.

"You promise me—" she said directly to me, but just then the show came back on, and Elvira once again became a statue who only moved to refill her cup every time it was empty. Of what happened on screen, I remember nothing more than the forest of rails and that frail little deer running away in a miniskirt. What I can remember is Elvira's voice at the end and her eyes filled with tears, I suppose because of the prospect of a whole week without Arnaldo, that loneliness that tasted like mint that she would have to drink in little sips.

"You promise me," she began again, and it seemed she needed to steady herself with another cup of peppermint liqueur, which by now must have been staining her blood green. "Promise me that you'll never . . . When you were very small your mother came with me to Paraná, in Entre Ríos, you know? We arrived there one afternoon to take back what was mine. Your mother stayed in the hotel while I went to the promenade along the river to see if I could catch him looking in her eyes the same way he looked in mine. I told your mother I knew where to find them . . . But that was a lie. All I knew was that she lived there and that he even went so far as renting a boat to take her out and kiss her on the mouth beneath the willow trees. Your mother waited for me in the hotel's tearoom, drawing *mburucuyá* flowers in a huge sketchbook. Your mother was excellent at drawing, did you know that?

I was determined to return to Buenos Aires with what was mine. But I had nothing, not even an address, not even a clue, nothing. Along the promenade nearly everyone was in a couple, and nearly all of them were eating fritters. Each stand had a line of people waiting, and I went up and down each one of them, certain I would find them. Someone had told me her name was Judith, and each time I saw a dark-haired woman buying more than one fritter, I approached in a friendly manner and asked, 'Are you Judith?'"

Elvira went silent, and it had been a while since she looked at me. She got up and switched off the television—all the expended light concentrated into a point at the exact center and then disappeared just as quickly as it had appeared. Elvira sat back down next to me and put her left arm around me, placing me on her lap of her sparking dressing gown. I stayed very still, partly out of fear of catching on fire and partly because I was uncomfortable; my body was twisted the wrong way, and when Elvira became serious like this she scared me.

"Someone told me that couples in the area would go to Bajada

Grande because there, at dusk, the sun lured the *surubí* fish up from the depths, and couples would kiss furtively in the light reflected up off their flanks in the river. I began to run, and after two blocks I realized I had no idea what direction I was running in or where I had left my wristwatch. I had no idea how long I had been there, and we had to catch a bus to go home. One afternoon was all the time I had to find them and to show him that I was capable of hanging on to him."

Elvira breathed in deeply and stayed quiet for a few seconds, and I made the most of the opportunity to get comfortable, sitting stiffly by her side without looking at her.

Then she bent down and whispered in my ear. "Never run off with a Sephardic Jewess," she said. "They bear the thirst of the desert in their bellies. They are such fiery women, they're like odalisques whose gaze men can't resist. The moment they hear the jingle of the coins on their skirts, the men turn and go to find them. And if they lie down together, you've lost—you can't compete with that. They're women who don't worry about falling pregnant, they have the thirst of the desert in their bellies. That's what a Jewess is, and because they come from no country, they live in tents in the middle of the desert, and they'll go anywhere to bewitch the men and take them away to build a nation and dominate the world. Look at what's happening here. Everything they gather up they take away with them, they're evil. Promise me . . ."

Elvira got rid of me and went to the bathroom. I got up to turn on the television, but after the point of light, there was only static. In a hurry I filled my cup up with peppermint liqueur and tried to drink it down in one gulp. It stung my tongue and tasted bitter and sweet at the same time, something for strange palates; until then all I had done was moisten my lips, and the act of drinking that little bit of color was what I loved. Sometimes it seemed that grown-ups consumed horrible things just to be able to get on with the world. I could understand coffee and yerba mate—I loved drinking yerba mate with milk and lots of sugar—but how could anyone truly enjoy whiskey or Cynar or Pineral or lit cigarettes? I thought that smoking was a sensual pleasure; I smoked menthol cigarettes that I stole from my uncle, and I smoked them without lighting up, they were delicious. It was a very complex activity that required a level of attention where you had to pretend to be distracted but actually give it your entire presence. I loved to smoke, and what's more, it gave me a reason to be alone, to shut myself in the bathroom and practice in front of the mirror.

The next thing I saw when I barely opened my eyes was my mother's neck as she carried me to the bedroom, to my bed. As soon as she saw I could rouse myself and begin asking questions, she said, "It's very late. Go to sleep because you have school tomorrow, and it's the big concert." I relaxed into her capable arms. I had become an expert in enjoying the fleeting things, the moments of true contact. The texture of my mother's jacket was different from that of her sweater, though I could feel both of them. The jacket smelled like blue, and one of its golden buttons, big and concave, pressed into my cheek. I loved that metal button, warming up as I rested my face against it.

The pressure from my palms was different from that of the fingers I was using to hold on, and it changed with each step, as I slipped a little. I loved just letting myself go on this short journey, hugging tightly to her and drifting to sleep. It was light at night, and I swung in my mother's arms with a movement from a time I couldn't quite remember, as if the best way I knew to rest was a kind of hammock in which I could lose control of myself and let myself fall without fear. There were different odors too: the warmest one was hers, an aroma I already knew, sweet and greasy, but her clothes smelled colder, waxier, like in an airport.

She took off my clothes and put on my pajamas, then tucked me in. "Stay a little while," I dared to ask. And so, in silence, she lay down next to me, still clothed and on top of the bed. She must have been tired because she fell asleep immediately, in the middle of my most absolute happiness, in the middle of my silent celebration: *My mama is spoiling me*.

I began to deploy innumerable strategies to avoid falling asleep; I wanted to be awake so I wouldn't miss a moment of it. I could barely move without waking this sleeping beauty, but the higher priority of my sleeping mother—although she was so close that she was as unsettling as a Picasso—was something I felt grateful for. Seeing my mother sleep was a complete happiness, but I had to remain calm, attentive, awake.

Everything I did to stay awake had an opposite effect, I had to change tactics quicker and quicker, and at some point my fatigue was so great that the only thing that occurred to me was to count sheep. Then I decided to think about wild beasts, about giant tigers crouching in the grass. I brought in wolves howling in the distance that could smell fear and were convinced of the success of their hunt. I saw the sheep giving in to this fear, paralyzed in the face of the vastness of the plains, certain they could not negotiate the wire fences due to their weakness. I saw one of the brave sheep become entangled in the fence, the barbed wire stuck in its wool, trapped in a position of escape, but calm, with the other sheep bleating around her. I saw the bewildered sheep run and launch themselves in a foolish attempt at escape. I saw them gather about the lambs, trying to hide them behind their spindly legs. The hyenas arrived, resigned to the hatred and disdain on which they were nurtured, moving around with clear laziness in the middle distance, prowling about tentatively, obeying the order of their scent, but prey also to the furrow of their obligation. I saw the mouths of the sheep bleating without air, muted noises as they went nobly toward the jaws, calm with their eyes open and their ears full of dull sounds, flesh against flesh, breath against breath. I saw how, their pupils dilated, they gazed without seeing the portrait of the entire night, bleating silently until they were just a stain of innards on a shared tableau.

I was woken by the foghorns of ships in the oceans of the night. It was something that fascinated me, that filled me with terror but also with a happy curiosity. It wasn't common for me to hear them because I wasn't usually awake at that hour. The first time I heard them, there were two of them, one shorter and one longer, and I realized I had heard them before but never noticed. But my ears clearly recognized them. I hesitated over whether this was real or a dream, so I looked around my room and took stock of all the things I came across. The die-cast Donald Duck hanging on the wall, a picture of the town hall from *Billiken* drawn on the inside of the belly of a giant bear that my mother had tacked to the wall in a fit of laughter, the huge closet opposite the bed, with the doors closed tight so that all the terror would stay inside, the curtains over the window into the laundry room, the desk with its huge lamp. Just as soon as I had taken inventory of all this, I became aware of the flat reality of it all, and I stopped to marvel at everything the dead of night had brought me.

After the first time I discovered this, if I remembered, I tried to go out and seek that nocturnal presence, but I could never outlast my fatigue, no matter how I tried. Fatigue and willpower didn't seem to be made of the same stuff. The more I tried to steel my will, the harder I set myself, the sooner I was at the mercy of my unconscious, and the sooner I fell asleep. Fatigue and willpower were materially dissimilar, strangers to each other, natural enemies.

Nonetheless, on the morning after I heard the foghorns, I never remembered them. The memory would come back through something else the day delivered, some fickle and meaningless detail that left me with a strange sensation, and after a long while, an inopportune prow appeared before me with its nocturnal cargo. If I recalled the darkness during the day, it filled me with fear, but if I woke up at night, I was delighted to be awake while everyone else slept.

The foghorns sounded deep and distant but clear and powerful. Where did those ships come from that left in the middle of the night? What port was so close to my house in the middle of all the cement, that in the deepest dark of the night, I could hear the somber trumpets of enormous ships?

From this open-eyed sleep I was woken by the cold. A cold that swam over me like a tide and froze me: I had wet the bed. It made me horribly sad that I had given in to a warmth that was now a frozen and shameful puddle. By luck my mother had managed to escape before the storm without me noticing. She was no longer in my bedroom. And the shame of my piss was ostensibly greater than that of her ruse, her mockery of my attempts to surveil her. She left me like that: alone in the nocturnal vastness of my bed, when it was dry.

I got up in the dark and took off the damp sheets. Then I had to plunge myself deep into the worst of the burning volcanoes;

I had to open the closet to fetch clean sheets. I'm not sure what I was afraid of most, opening the portal of terror or being inside there in complete solitude, undertaking the task almost in slow motion to avoid making noises that might wake my mother.

I bundled the dirty sheets and hid them under my bed, unfolded the fresh ones, and stretched them out as best I could. I had to do it as quickly as possible to escape the darkness and sink back into sleep, begging the gods not to let me glaze myself again in that sweet syrup, releasing the moorings of my bladder in the middle of the high sea of the night.

I don't remember the date, but that day the morning routine was special. My mother did everything as if in a rush, and she seemed happy. She had made me a costume for the school concert; we were going to sing "*Que se vengan los chicos*," a song that says "some who were from Venus, they say, brought the Three Marias as a gift." I was chosen to be in a group of aliens that arrived on a rocket made from cardboard and glazed metallic paper. That glazed paper was so wonderful—when you cut it with scissors you could hear the crackling of the aluminum particles. Then you'd cover it with glue and stick it to your drawing in art class. It made me feel like a goldsmith, a man with a unique task.

The costume that my mother had managed to put together—Ms. Zulema had pasted a little notice into our notebooks with instructions about how we should dress—consisted of a black headband that she used to keep her hair from her face, two knitting needles wrapped in gold paper, and two pompoms made from cotton balls, glued together, to make the antennae. The rest of the costume was just my sky-blue suit. I'm not sure if my mother didn't have time to find the plain white T-shirt and blue shorts from the instructions or if she just wanted me to look elegant, presentable.

The problem with the headband was that the knitting needles, my mother's substitute for a lighter metal, were too heavy and wouldn't stay up on their own. They each slipped down to one side, so I looked like a little bug in a blue suit with dark socks and laced shoes, a sort of insect from the movies that my mother found adorable.

Back then I couldn't understand why my mother wanted me to be special, standing out from the others, visibly different. I just wanted to be an alien, someone who could look to the sky when referring to his family, completely naturally.

Her idea of the alien, however, was much more earthbound, like those ladybugs that could make her happy by their mere presence, no matter what was going on around her.

It would have given me so much pleasure to stick black and white spots on my back and flit my wings nearby to surprise her in the middle of her somber expressions, cleansing her face with a smile that reinforced the possibility of her ideals.

To remedy the effect of the drooping antennae, my mother told me to hold them with my hands to keep them upright throughout the performance.

I loved the song we were going to sing. It was full of intergalactic friendship, and it named without euphemism creatures from Venus, from Mars, people who could turn themselves into a promise. Who knows, amid so much diversity there could be quiet and obedient little boys who dreamed about Astro Boy, full of fear, just like in that episode where they give him a human heart.

I was delighted to take part in the concert, but the song was clearly written by an adult. The entire image of an alien humanity was annihilated by the impact of the corrective meteorite of the lyric that said, “Everybody’s welcome to my birthday party, and don’t worry about bringing gifts.” What child could be so perverse that they could feign the hypocrisy of worldly indifference and happily sing that nobody should worry about the only important thing?

Behind the scenes, the wait was a delightful jitteriness. Those of us awaiting our entrance were calm, and those who were about to step off the precipice into performance were in a tightly controlled race against time, ready to begin the concert.

The performance space was enormous, with a giant stage where, from time to time, theater companies put on shows with ancient actors and actresses that our parents recognized as radio stars of the past. It was *enormous*.

The alien song was a fairly important part of the concert, and what we had to do seemed easy from the crowd. But to actually perform the song was horrendously complicated. Our lively number was a proposition worthy of a UNICEF plenary session: the final message we sought to impart as educators was that there was room for all and a horn of plenty on our planet.

Carrying the cardboard rocket, we five aliens had to enter via the side of the stage, like those ballerinas who dance along on their toes, everyone’s head looking one way, then the other, their hands linked, leaping in that ridiculous but perfect *Swan Lake* way. We had to make our way to the middle, the proscenium, and sing out loud while the earthlings, the living trees, and all the crepe paper fauna in creation gathered around us with looks of fascination as they hung wreaths of flowers around our necks, as if instead of aliens we were swingers who had just arrived in Hawaii.

In one fateful moment during the wait, the realization of an imminent disaster dawned upon me, and I was left aghast. I went more silent—silent even for me. If I had to hold up the nose of the cardboard rocket, I wouldn't be able to hold my antennae upright.

The spaceship, on its side and held at waist height, was completely weightless, but even though one hand was enough to stop it from dropping, I still needed two hands to stop my Martian from becoming a bug with floppy antennae.

The sensation of imminence overwhelmed me; there was nothing I could do to prevent something that hadn't even happened yet, and in any case, knowing it was about to happen made me feel worse than the event itself. Not only would I not pull off the role of an alien, I would surely end up as a clumsy insect who would crash the spaceship.

Ms. Zulema looked like a little girl. Her cheeks were rosier than usual, and she was standing next to us, her eyes darting back and forth, rooted to the spot and repressing in vain her exaggerated nerves. In her heeled moccasins she couldn't help shuffling toward the entrance to the stage in little steps that made us shuffle forward too. At one point she noticed me and said, "Hold those antennae straight, would you?" Luckily she turned away just then and didn't see that by straightening my antennae I dropped the nose of the spaceship. Luckily she turned around again and looked at me with an expression that I knew would save me. Without a single word and without disturbing me, with the clear logic of a calculated chess move, she took me from the first position and put me in third, right in the middle of the rocket. She looked at me sweetly and said, "Hold up your antennae." My lip began to quiver, and I wanted to go to the bathroom.

Suddenly something changed in the atmosphere, as if all the air had been drawn away in a single breath that left us dry and then just as quickly returned to blast in our faces. First we could hear a murmur run through the audience, then the sound of motors stopping, and then shouting. Onstage the music continued playing, but we all stood still, and for a few moments everyone looked around wide-eyed. From the depths of the hall the murmurings began to crackle, like a fledgling flame that begins to grow because everything it touches is flammable. In just a few seconds the whole room was a wildfire of voices struggling to escape closed mouths, like a mumbling that couldn't quite be understood but seemed capable of burning down the entire concrete structure of the school.

When the noise reached the stage, everything began to change and without knowing exactly how the murmurings became audible words, a sentence: "Bomb threat."

The school principal went up onstage and began to speak into the microphone, but the noise of footsteps and chairs scraping was so loud, she didn't even realize it wasn't switched on and nobody was listening to her because everyone was trying to move toward the exit in a kind of silent panic, in case their fiery voices lit the fuse to the promised dynamite. My eyes scanned the crowd for my mother's head or the blue lapels and gold buttons of her coat. Maybe she hadn't arrived at the concert on time, or the tide of bodies had dragged her to the exit like so many of the other parents who wanted to head back toward the stage to scoop their children up into the safety of their arms. I was dizzied by the silence, by the power of my eyes in the search for that blue jacket, those golden buttons in a sea of corduroy, duffel coats, wide belts, sandals and wigs, of turquoise bell-bottoms, cream-colored jackets, ties with knots as big as a pigeon, of miniskirts and tightly fitting boots with zippers on the side that went all the way up the calf to the knees.

The color drained from her cheeks, Ms. Zulema aged instantly, and I have no idea how but she kept us in line, moving us toward the side exit, firm and patient but effective enough to march us to the sidewalk without dispersing us. I remember the image of her acting perfectly, and I am still deafened by the silence with which she took charge of us, a silence that stood out among the general silence, like a deep and warm river that flows into the cold ocean and resists as long as it can before melding into the indifference of the greater body of water.

We were gathered on the sidewalk, along with the police cars and the fire engines. We were like the inhabitants of a province that waits in a public space to hear of the immediate future of its territory, threatened by a litany of forces of nature. I never felt that way again. In that moment there was no hierarchy: kids, teachers, mothers, fathers, secretaries: all of us could be blown away in an instant.

From amid the crowd of overcoats I caught sight of a gold flash approaching. And then another. The blue wool moved toward me like a child moves toward their last chance to ring the bell for a free ride on the merry-go-round. A very beautiful young woman ran and fixed her brown eyes on mine, eyes full of anguish that had been devoured by a conflict that I wouldn't understand until many years later. I could explode, become a cluster of particles in the air around me, a brunette was running toward me even if she was taking a long time, even if she never arrived, even if she never existed.

When every last one of us from the school was gathered on the sidewalk, a small group of firemen and police gathered near the entrance, and one of them used a megaphone to inform us it was a false alarm. It was all he said, a kind of password that lowered the tension immediately and caused the mass of bodies to disengage, as if we'd been contained in an inflatable swimming pool that punctures and begins to leak water until it is empty. Everyone went home. I've always wondered what happened to the cardboard rocket.

On the way home, my mother stopped at a kiosk and bought me some candy: a Holanda chocolate bar, a Jack, and three Topolino lollipops that came with a little toy. For herself she chose mandarin-flavored heart-shaped candies that she opened right there as we were walking, taking one after the after as if they were Seconal pills. So much candy—and above all the promise of the little toys that came with the Topolinos, that looked like tiny fetuses that I adored for some reason—confirmed that something very serious had happened.

My mother always tried to keep me away from candy; she said sweet things contained parasites and that parasites were the worst of the worst and that's why she drank her yerba mate bitter, not like her cousins who added sweetener and were a pair of morons.

The question of the parasites was complicated because beyond the threat of becoming a moron myself, I knew very well what my mother was talking about. At that age I already hated the *ñandú*, and every now and again I thought about how it was a blessing to live in a city that distanced me from a possible meeting with one of those monstrous ostrichlike birds, which, according to my mother, were the type of sissies that bury their heads in the sand at the first sign of danger. One time, in the countryside in the south of Buenos Aires province where we were spending a few days on vacation, Uncle Rodolfo took me to inspect the grounds with two of his farmhands. We were traveling in an old pickup truck, on a voyage that could have been lifted from a safari film if not for the monotony of the countryside. But to tell the truth, the pickup truck made a lot of noise, and the sun was exhausting, and the bumps from the vehicle's nonexistent suspension meant there was no way to relax. At one point one of the farmhands yelled—in the distance he had spotted a flock of *choikes,* as he called them, and my uncle almost stopped the pickup before swinging it around and driving slowly in the direction of the huge birds. At a certain point we stopped, my uncle turned off the motor, motioned for me to be completely silent, and then we got out noiselessly and posted up on the port side of our armored battleship. The *ñandú* birds stopped grazing, extended their necks, and looked over expectantly in our direction without moving, and then I suppose because they saw us so far away, they went right back to grazing in the same greedy, indolent manner of cows.

I thought the plan was to approach on foot, calm and silent so they wouldn't be scared away, but the farmhand who had spied them pulled out a revolver with a wooden handle and a thin barrel, steadied his aim by resting the gun on his left forearm, and opened fire. It was so quick that I didn't even have time to take fright, because in the same instant one of the sissy birds fell straight to the ground, and the rest of them, in a reckless and foolish stampede, ran off hysterically in all directions, as if fleeing in such a flat terrain without any shelter could be anything other than a futile task.

My uncle and the farmhands whooped victoriously and began to walk in the direction of the dead bird. I straggled a few paces behind, but then I began to walk in time with Uncle Rodolfo's whistling. When we arrived at the animal, the killer crouched down, grabbed it by the head, looked at it, and smiled. "I got it in the head," he said. "The bullet must have gone in through the eye."

My uncle leaned down—that slight gesture made the farmhand stand up straightaway and cede his place—then began to go over the bird with a serious expression and began to move it to show me each part of the animal and to tell me about the birds and how they lived, how they fit into the landscape of the Argentine gaucho and the native Indians.

"A man must prepare himself, study hard, and get to know the land and the condition his fellow countrymen live in," he said very seriously while the farmhands stood behind me, waiting for God knows what.

When he had finished talking, he motioned to the other farmhand, who drew a knife hanging from his belt and moved decisively toward the animal. My uncle got up and stood behind me, taking me by the shoulders and pushing me a few steps closer to the gray bird, which was smaller than I expected and was covered in dirty feathers that seemed to have nothing at all to do with the ostriches that I had seen in my book, *Questions and Answers for Curious Boys*. Everything in the countryside seemed washed over with a gray poverty; it all seemed much smaller than in the stories my uncle told, much more lost in an exaggeratedly extensive terrain, much less colorful.

A man should know his land, my uncle's serious advice echoed in my head, but this wasn't my land—my land was the worn-out parquetry of my bedroom. In this land a farmhand was slicing open the stomach of a stupid bird with clean strokes.

I had no time to react and I found it difficult to believe that the bird would let itself be treated so, without screaming, without any resistance, completely at the mercy of the bullet of the man who discovered it.

I looked around to see if one of its relatives was watching us or rounding up a feathered and vengeful posse, which of course would come and take me away, or if the other birds remained to keep vigil over their fallen companion. But there was nothing, the sissy bird was all alone, or else I couldn't see the hidden flock on a pampa so linear that there were no hiding places at all.

A shout from the man with the knife and the laughter of the other farmhand and my uncle brought me urgently back to the scene. The dead bird displayed its insides without any modesty and from within came a ball of writhing white worms, almost as big as the stomach itself of the animal, which twisted and squirmed like the fleeing birds, and if it had vocal cords would have deafened us with its screams of terror. Disgust and horror can be the same thing: I learned that right there, in the Argentine countryside, beneath a pale sky in a puddle of pampa blood.

That's where I learned about the parasites that my mother hated, one of the images I would have preferred to erase from my mind, an image I would have preferred never to have seen.

The writhing ball steadily lost its vitality, and the knife once again took center stage, the farmhand shredding the belly of the gutted bird and scraping the chunks of meat to remove the nest of eggs that filthy medusa of worms had undoubtedly sown.

His companion, in the meantime, unfolded a cloth he'd

fetched from the pickup truck. They put the chunks of meat on it, and the butcher said to my uncle, "It's not worth taking the wings, they're as tough as leather. We might as well leave them to the vultures."

"Do *ñandú* birds eat a lot of candy?" I asked as we walked along. The three men laughed, and my uncle intoned to me again his knowledge about country cooking and the responsibility of killing.

"You only kill to eat, now we'll ask Miss Sara to make us *milanesas* out of the *picana*, the sirloin cap on the animal's rump." And that's how I came to know about parasites and how I first heard that terrible word *picana*.

The first thing I saw when we got home was our little Christmas tree, as tiny as an old pony. My mother had put it up while I was at school at the final rehearsal, but she hadn't said anything to me, so it would be a surprise. Our little tree looked like it was growing in the middle of the lonely pampa; there was no manger, and my mother got nervous when I pointed out that our nativity scene had no baby Jesus, no cows or donkeys, no bright star, or even a virginal young maiden or an older carpenter. The tension that came over my mother when I asked for a more traditional celebration—just like the Eucharist that I closed my mouth over, the host that seals the lips of the faithful Christian on his knees—was what made me stay silent.

Our little tree was quite sparse, and instead of tinsel and baubles we had homemade decorations: little drawings of mine and little knitted figures that my mother had bought in a regional handicrafts store. It was very close to Christmas Eve, and that was the only reference we would need. I no longer insisted upon affirming the historical truth of the event, to save myself a lecture about a world of starving children, about how the real celebration was being together, and that in reality, the origins of this birth nearly two thousand years ago was the most scandalous lie in the history of the Western world.

What could be so wrong about getting together to eat chicken, open presents, and to think, for just a moment, that the arrival of the kingdom of God is possible? But I thought of this in total silence, avoiding the discursive rage of the lady of the house.

My mother asked me to take off my little blue suit, to give back her headband and the knitting needles, and to put on my pajamas, because we would be spending the afternoon at home.

She curled up on the sofa, wrapped herself in the red poncho she used for a blanket, and sat watching the little rays of afternoon sun that streaked through the whole apartment.

"I'll fix you some milk later," she said without looking at me. I went to my bedroom to open up the Jack and the Topolinos on top of my bed. Inside the Jack chocolate bar was a figurine of the witch, Cachavacha, and the lollipop packages had a green car with poorly molded wheels, a little figurine whose expression and purpose were impossible to discern, and an olive-green monkey. I gathered them all up in a pile on the blue mattress with the intention of inventing a game, but I gave up almost immediately. The links between a primate, a green car, and a witch that makes children disappear were so improbable that I knocked them away and opened the closet to look for my Goliath cannon. If I'd had any more of the gunpowder caps left I would have passed the evening shooting the cannon at those irreconcilable surprise toys. Instead, I had to use my imagination to shoot at everything, my little bronze cannon leaving the world in flames.

The days that followed were strange. My mother was more

and more serious, and she sat on the sofa with her feet tucked beneath her during the day until the night transformed it into her bed, without reading, in silent concentration. She got up very carefully to make me something to eat or to help me with one of my more difficult homework exercises or to sweep up. In the living room there was a woolen rug, like a long beard that formed a warm and gray lawn that didn't quite reach the walls. My mother brushed it from the center outward and then swept the uncovered parquetry. If I was nearby, drinking my milk or watching an episode of Astro Boy or playing with my stickers. I couldn't stop watching the way she swept—the sensation overwhelmed me. I don't know why this activity captivated me. From my vantage point it was normal to see the imperfections in my mother's task, the tiny mounds of dirt that she left behind, the spots she missed without realizing. From her height, she lost the perfect vision of the floor she was sweeping that I could see.

"Stop pointing it out to me, stop showing me where I'm missing spots. Mind your own business! Do your homework, and let me do mine!" She burst out one time, the last time.

On one of those afternoons, Uncle Rodolfo came over. It was a long time since I'd seen him, and he was different: his sideburns were thicker and he'd let his mustache grow long. He pressed the doorbell twice and then after a while knocked on the apartment door before opening it with his keys. My uncle usually came over with a pile of Suchard chocolate blocks, one of each flavor, and another pile of Milkybars, just as big. I loved chocolate, and I loved how his visits provided me with this drug that made my mother mad and caused her to warn me about the toxic effects of devouring all the little blocks of chocolate and the Milkybars in one sitting. The theme of the parasites was a serious one; my mother was firm and unwavering when she spoke of it.

That evening my uncle didn't bring me anything. When I heard him arrive I ran from my bedroom to the living room to greet him, and I found him with a grave expression. He greeted me rather hurriedly and then looked at my mother and said to her with a cold fury that he had been waiting over the road for a long time but the shutters were down. My mother jolted awake all at once, jumping up off the sofa, and then she told me to go to my room, that she was going to prepare some yerba mate for my uncle and that they were going to have a grown-up talk.

I stayed in my room trying to figure out what it was they would speak about in a grown-up talk, what sort of things a child couldn't hear. I had already seen a *ñandú* gutted with a knife, a colony of blind snakes that died moments after being removed from their home in the insides of the bird, I had dreamed of hyenas and the prohibited sweets of the Casa Suiza Patisserie, someone had threatened to blow up my school before the friendly aliens could arrive. I already knew that children all over the world with bloated bellies died from starvation, that I should never ask about my father, and that baby Jesus was a miserable liar for whom people stole and murdered. What topic of conversation was inappropriate for my age?

A few minutes later I heard Uncle Rodolfo leaving and my mother entering the bathroom. With the door open, she washed her face with cold water and tied her hair in a ponytail. In a rush she put on the coat with the gold buttons and told me she needed to go out, that she would see if Elvira was in and could look after me while she was gone.

Elvira didn't answer the door, neither the doorbell nor the anxious knocking of my mother, who came back, sobbed in front of me, and said, "I can't take you with me."

In no time at all she wiped away her tears, two solitary tears, one from each eye, turned on the television at very low volume, sat me down on the sofa, wrapped me up in the poncho, and told me to watch my cartoons. She told me that I shouldn't get up for any reason at all and if the doorbell rang I shouldn't answer and that I shouldn't open the door for anyone. Not even Elvira. She emptied the can where we kept our savings, kissed me on the forehead, went out, and turned each of the two locks on our door twice. She never locked up so much.

It was almost nightfall when I was left alone. What cartoons could I watch? The programs at that hour were for grown-ups, and the news reports scared me. I unwound myself from the poncho in a dangerous act of disobedience, got up from the sofa, and went to the kitchen. I took a little bread roll from the bag behind the door, then went to the fridge and took out the butter dish, and got a knife and the sugar bowl. I went back to the living room, breaking the bread in half and spreading it with butter and sugar. I changed the channel and became hypnotized, sitting on the edge of the living room table, a few centimeters away from the screen.

My mother wasn't long in coming home. Much sooner than I expected she came in, shut the door, and leaned against it, her eyes swollen. She stayed like that for a while, and with the sound of the television in the background, she seemed to be asleep with her eyes open, less agitated but more tired. Then she woke up suddenly and walked across the room to the bookshelf, taking down the tin full of our savings. She put her hand in her pocket and took out the fistful of bills and put it back in the tin. From her other pocket she took my bankbook from the National Savings and Insurance Fund and put that back in the tin too. I hadn't noticed that she took it, and I felt a mix of indignation and sorrow, but I didn't say anything. I was still trying to capture the breeze of my mother's passing, but the air didn't have that metallic odor it normally did after one of my mother's outings. I tried to breathe in deeply without her noticing; for me it was a very intimate act, a way of embracing her without showing dependence. That time the air around her just smelled of air, nothing special.

She lowered the shutters completely, and the little rays of light that came in at that time of the evening from the streetlight went dark.

On TV they were showing some red-pelted animals in the snow in some place near Alaska, their eyes half-shut against the wind, gathered next to a bare, black tree. The ground was white and the sky was white. The camera focused in on the head of one of the huge bison. It was calm, awake, covered in frost. Stalactites of frozen mucus hung from its nostrils, and, to me, its expression seemed strange, as if its despair had passed through the state of panic and it was simply waiting for the moment when its internal mechanics would stop. Like a soldier trained to be steadfast, for the obligation to resist without freezing, for the unlikely promise of a sliver of springtime that would bring the thaw, that would redress so much suffering, so much injustice.

My mother went to the kitchen and came back with two glasses of hot Nesquik. She sat next to me on the table to watch TV and gave me one of the glasses, then drank from hers. How disgusting! How could she drink hot Nesquik and pretend that the curdled milk on top is an easily avoidable obstacle? I left my glass on the tray and began to nibble around the edges of a cookie. I loved to eat cookies in tiny bites, gnawing away at the edges like a guinea pig or a squirrel. At one point my mother gave me one of those looks like she was going to start with one of her *Why do people ask for Nesquik, cookies, and everything else under the sun?* lectures, but when our eyes met, hers turned to water, and instead of scolding me, she hugged me and sat there in silence watching the people watching us from above the bison. Behind the television was the bookcase, and on one of the shelves, leaning against the spines of the books, there was a row of rag dolls with inscriptions on their bellies along the lines of *Don't Leave* or *A Star Is Born*, and they stared us down with their plastic eyes. They sat there side by side, their shoulders slumped and a look of stubbornness on their faces that defied their consignment to that shelf. For a long time I tried to figure out the complete sentence that could be formed with the words on those rag dolls, to figure out what hidden message we couldn't decipher, my mother and I, while we watched TV or gazed at the rising sun or the pink of its setting as it filtered in rays from the gaps in the shutters at dusk. But all I can remember now are those two phrases: *Don't Leave* and *A Star Is Born*.

When my mother turned her gaze back to the television I summoned the courage to ask her, "What happened?"

She waited a few seconds and responded with a question of her own. "What do you say we go to the kitchen and make some bangers and mash?"

I cackled with glee and my mother stood up, loaded the two glasses and the tea towel onto the tray, and said, "Go on then, you bring the cookies, and we'll start cooking."

In the kitchen the whole atmosphere changed. While my mother saw to the boiling water for the sausages, she suggested that I prepare the mashed potatoes. I opened the box, read the instructions out loud, and then got out everything I needed: milk, butter, water, a cup, and a pot. When the food was ready we put out the place mats, the cutlery, and the breadbasket, and we sat down opposite each other. We were happy and hungry. In fact

I just felt like eating—it was unusual for me to be hungry, and it was unusual for me to remember to eat or to feel like interrupting what I was doing to sit down in front of a plate of food.

Full of enthusiasm, my mother chatted away about any old thing, and all of it seemed entertaining to me. I delighted in these conversations in which I barely spoke a word except to ask her to be more specific about some detail or another, especially things about her childhood, which she never usually spoke about.

She took out the bottle of Crespi table wine and poured me half a glass, then she looked at me as if she were about to speak, but stopped. A few seconds later she jumped up from the table and put on her blue coat, told me she'd be right back, and left the apartment with her hair out. I was left alone in the kitchen watching the vapor rise from the sausages on my plate, playing with the mashed potatoes with my fork. At one point I heard footsteps approaching in the hallway, and I stayed very quiet to see if it was my mother returning. By the door of our apartment the footsteps stopped, and I heard nothing more. Whoever it was, they were just on the other side of the door, and for a moment I was scared. I stood, grateful that I was in socks so I could sneak up without making any noise. I went into the living room and stared down the door, breathing very lightly and taking great care that I moved without the slightest noise. I stood there not knowing what to do. After a while it seemed that the feet on the other side of the door were moving, and I wanted to run away, but then I heard the sound of the key in Elvira's door and her squeaky voice that said: "Where's my Ñatita? Mommy's home! Guess what Mommy brought you today!" Just then the door shut, and I never found out what surprise awaited the old and blind dog, curled up in a ball on the sofa.

I ran back and sat down at the table, and there was no longer any steam rising from the sausages, but I could hear the footsteps of my mother returning. Before she even finished opening the door I heard her asking me, "Guess what I brought you?" She had run to the kiosk to buy me a bottle of Mirinda soda. "We have to make a toast, and if I have some wine you can't say 'chin-chin' with water."

We toasted, ate the cold bangers and hardened mash, but we never stopped chatting the whole time. After an apple for dessert my mother made some coffee and poured herself a cup, then returned to the table and lit a cigarette. There was something special about that night that made us feel comfortable and willing, as if instead of the kitchen we were seated at Bambi, or Casa Suiza, or the Steinhauser Café, and instead of bangers and mash, we had eaten fancy charcuterie and a sticky frangipane cake made from aromatic almonds.

I watched her smoke, and she seemed to strike up conversations with invisible companions. She arched her eyebrows, touched her hair, let out the first mouthfuls of smoke like ample responses and interspersed them with tendrils of smoke that billowed out her nose, as if supporting or retracting arguments in an internal discussion. I began to hold my breath again, I didn't want to miss a single detail of this beautiful young woman in front of me, conversing comfortably in silence, her lips moist, notably sexy and daring, and for one night—in a way she hadn't been in a long time—relaxed.

"What are you laughing about?" she asked when she saw me laughing at the mere sight of her. I wasn't in the least surprised, and she just pulled her hair to one side and returned to her internal discussion with full knowledge that I was admiring her.

I promised to myself I would smoke. I would wait as many years as necessary, but in that moment I understood that I had given myself over to the notion that I would only become an adult through smoking.

I was delighted to see her like that, and I didn't mind that she was talking to other men—it was obvious that she was talking to other men—her eyes shone, and her smile changed from shy to cheeky and easy, and her hair opened darkly like one of those nocturnal carnivorous flowers only known to the souls of the desert.

I must have fallen asleep at the table with my arms crossed, the plates to one side, because I remember nothing more of that night that I'll never forget, that night that stays with me like a precious gemstone shining for me, and me alone.

To whom could I explain the extraordinary sensuality of a meal of cold sausages or the smoke from 43 70 cigarettes?

I saw the light of the lamp on the nightstand and realized I was awake. I had no idea what time it could be, but I knew it must be very late; the foghorns always came in the small hours. I got up and walked very quietly across the parquetry toward the living room and when I got there I found her reading.

"Mama, can you hear the ocean liners?" She left her copy of *The Manipulated Man* to one side and looked at me. From the ashtray on the table, her cigarette sent out a smoke signal that rose in a perfectly straight line.

"What are you doing out of bed at this hour?" she replied.

The same old dynamic as always, she always answered my questions with a question of her own.

"Can you hear the foghorns, Mama?" I insisted.

"What foghorns are you talking about?" she replied.

I put my head down and began to turn around to go back to my bedroom, to get back into bed.

"No, my love, no. That's not a ship."

"Yes, it is, it's a boat. Can't you hear it?"

"No, my love, it's the train." She held me back. "You know how sometimes we pass the railway crossing at the station about twelve blocks away, the crossing at Ferro, you know? It's not a boat, my love, it's the train that goes to Moreno, and at this time of night there's hardly any noise because everyone is asleep, that's why you can hear the whistle from the locomotive. During the day it's impossible because of all the noise."

"Oh, you mean the railway crossing that Solita runs through," I said almost to myself, as quickly as I could, while I shuffled back to bed.

"What?" I heard my mother say as she switched on her lamp.

"*Pobre diabla,*" I said in silence and darkness.

I would have preferred not to know. I would have preferred the answer to be a question, like all the other times. I would have liked my mother to have guessed that this was exactly the question that she shouldn't answer for me. I would have liked her to know that I wanted to think there was a boat in the middle of the night, that the foghorns told me there was something else beyond, after all the oceans that separated us from the world. Even if you had to leave the port in the dead of night, I wanted to think that the darkness itself was my safety, my passport to a daytime port, where the sunshine glimmered like smiles I hadn't seen in the longest time, the kind of smile that flashes until it consumes itself without measure or fear, a wake on the high sea of a trusting face. I would have preferred to think it was possible to save, to spend years pasting stamps into my bankbook so that finally I could go up to the little window and purchase two tickets, one for her and one for me. In the end I would be like a bison gifting my coins to the snow so my savings would blossom like the springtime, and we would climb up the deck of an ocean liner holding hands, on a rope ladder suspended in the night air over the dark water, on our way to a daybreak in Mexico, in Spain, in Finland. The foghorns themselves would bear us along, sinking and darkening into the depths, then in the next swell bringing up to the surface those silvery sequins that would take us to the next sunny port. Together. Safe.

When I got up the next morning my mother was tidying the bookcase. She had washed her face, and her hair was tied back in a ponytail. I said good morning but she didn't respond. I went to the bathroom to brush my teeth and then to the kitchen to make myself a Nesquik. I delighted in putting two heaping soup spoonfuls into the glass, but with such an excessive amount I had to make sure that my mother wasn't watching. Then I had to pour the milk down the side with the glass tilted, so that it wouldn't disturb the chocolate layer. The milk would be tinged slightly with flavor but in the depths lay the thick mud, the destination I had to reach, the prize I had to earn. I loved to peer through the glass and inspect the marine landscape of peaks and troughs and, beneath the surface of the liquid, the paleness of dry earth. Only the line of contact held the dark brown coloring from the fusing of the elements.

I had to drink carefully, because to maintain that topography required a certain stability, and as the minutes went by the bedrock could be infiltrated, the liquid could permeate the upper layer, and then it was just a matter of time before everything mixed together and everything was lost.

My mother kept picking out books from the bookcase, and, before tossing them to the ground, she would empty them of dried flowers, postcards, and letters written on silky yellowed paper, stained with the blue ink of calligraphy.

What was written in those letters? I wondered. If they were from people who were now dead, what would those letters say about the time when they were written, about the authors they had survived?

Perched on a painter's ladder she thumbed through the books as if remembering; she wore that grave expression that was familiar to me, the one that said she wasn't available to anyone.

I went back to my Nesquik and saw that on one of the promontories, a trough, one of the largest ones, had begun to leak. I remembered something Ms. Zulema had told us: the deepest marine trench in the world was found in the Mariana Islands, in the northwest of the Pacific Ocean. It was eleven thousand meters deep.

"What?" I'd asked in the middle of geography class. I had heard perfectly well—I understood completely each of the words Ms. Zulema had used to weave her sentence. The teacher repeated the information for me. "The deepest marine trench . . ."

"What?" I said again, unable to contain myself.

"Did you not hear or can you not understand when you are spoken to?" replied my teacher.

I asked the same thing again, short and simple, but silently, just to myself. It left me perplexed to think that people kept on living in the face of monstrous things they could never face up to, things that could swallow them whole, carry them off into the darkness without even the remotest chance of survival. If that trench began to suck downward, what body could flail strongly enough to reach the surface? And if that bedrock was infiltrated? What if the very ocean itself began to seep through a crack? If that bewildering mass of water could wash away entire continents, what would happen to us? Would we all be sucked away?

"What?" I said in a low voice and finished my milk in one huge gulp, holding my breath as the sweet mud from the bottom of the glass began to reach my tongue.

I myself had swum in the sea, not in the Mariana Islands, of course, although it was all part of the ocean. On a family vacation in Miramar, I was enjoying the beach, and my mother insisted I go in the water with her. I ran up to the sea ready to deliver myself but when I arrived at the shoreline I was left petrified by the sight of the horizon, where the ocean meets the sky. I stood there for a few moments until my excitement came back and I looked all around me, at the people enjoying the waves that crashed about their feet, at their happy faces. *There's no danger,* I'd told myself. *Everybody is getting in.*

But my feet were trapped by the sight of the horizon and the certainty that out there, those people wouldn't be much help. "I'm not going to surrender myself to that hole," I said. I saw the vacationers moving toward that Goliath with smiles on their lips and my voice repeated its calm and desperate diatribe: "No."

But my mother led the counterattack. Standing on the sand and staring at her, I resisted. "I'm not going back into that hole."

She spun around and disappeared—she stopped watching me and slipped under the sea. But after a while, just like Venus, her head emerged in almost the same place, a sequence of events that turned me into a reciter of psalms, into a rabbi drowned in his own psychotic chanting: *Come back up, come back up, come back up.*

When I finished the Nesquik, I went to the living room to watch her. I sat on the sofa while she remained on the painter's ladder pulling out notes from inside her books. She opened them, read them a little, then pulled out all sorts of things I had no idea were inside there and seemed much more interesting than the texts of the books themselves. It was disturbing to see how the books had clutches of secret information inside that I didn't know about; they seemed like top secret spies who were waiting like sleeper agents for a sign that would wake them, and that could be deadly to the world as we know it.

What did I care about the fantastical lies told on the printed pages of the books? I wanted the secret story dried up in the petals of that flattened rose, on the autographed tickets from a theater in Stockholm, on that receipt with so many zeros that I couldn't tell if it was from Argentina or some strange continent, on those notes to people whose names I'd never heard. For me, next to this literature of unknown hands and signs that could become a part of the torrent of my blood, the other stuff, the typeset stories, were like tombstones stacked neatly in an ordered cemetery against the wall.

Why did my mother love books so much? Why did she declare her love with such school spirit? What did she think books could give me, or what could they free her from giving me?

In one of her readings, in one of those moments where she stopped what she was doing and stood there as if she had climbed a hilltop to give herself over to a letter she had been waiting months to receive, she saw me watching her and changed her expression. With her right hand she loosened the tie that held her hair back in a ponytail, relaxed her brow, and moistened her lips, almost imperceptibly. I took the opportunity to sink deeper into the sofa and lean into the backrest with my legs crossed.

Until that moment I had been perched on the edge, ready to dash off if she noticed me watching her and became angry.

"Do you want to know what it says?"

"Yes," was my only response.

She read a poem written by hand on the first page of the book she was holding, a poem that I remember ended with the line, *In the molten wind, will you recognize me?*

When she had finished reading she turned her face to me with a careless smile, too careless for the unease awoken in me by intrigue.

"I want to know who wrote that for you, who gave you that book. Was it a boyfriend?"

"Don't you want to know who it was that wrote such a sad poem?"

"No, I don't."

"Is that how you answer me?"

"I want to know who gave you that book, who copied that poem out for you, what he said to you. Why did he give you that book? Why did he copy it out for you? Was it a boyfriend?—

"And who said the poem was copied out for me?"

Right at that moment the doorbell rang, and I automatically ran to see who it was. My mother yelled for me to ask who it was before I opened the door, but the end of her sentence arrived when Elvira and her floral nightgown were already standing before us.

"May I come in?" She mixed her convent-school education with a worried gesture, exactly the type of manners that made my mother nervous.

"The rain in Spain stays mainly in the plain," my mother

would say, after our neighbor had left, elongating the vowel sounds as if instead of complimenting her, she was drowning her in the Baltic Sea for being so vulgar.

And Elvira, any time Ñata's breathing changed or she gave a whimper or barked at an unexpected moment, would change her entire body language and take on an expression of panic, as if she were barefoot and east of Java at the very moment the molten blanket of Krakatoa began to flow and turn into a burning carpet. Whenever she heard a sign like that coming from her apartment, Elvira stopped what she was doing midconversation and rushed back to check on Ñatita, who would be barely alive on the sofa, wrapped up in her pink crocheted woolen blanket, watched over by the doll dressed as a bride on the cotton tulle doily sitting on top of the television, and the Virgin on the sideboard, who perhaps made the most of the solitude to undertake the promised changing of colors, letting layer after layer of clothing drop to her feet until she was just down to her bra and panties, alone with the secret of her indecent but discreet conscience.

One time my mother worked up the courage to criticize her; she told her she was being melodramatic, that there was nothing wrong with the dog, and that it was just a dog anyway.

Elvira frightened me then—she went deep red and completely silent. It seemed like the veins on her neck would explode, and she began to cry suddenly, fat tears rolling down her cheeks, and she had to hold her jaw because it was trembling, and little howls slipped out, like from a beast in a muzzle. Elvira always had a handkerchief on hand, a little embroidered one that she carried around hidden up the sleeve of her jacket so that she would always be ready for the role of damsel in distress. But this crying fit turned out to be more like a fit of rage, a wall of impotence that required nothing more than that to make my mother understand her error, her lack of pity. But that crying fit also made Elvira part of our family, and Ñata, with her eyes almost as white as the Niagara Falls, became one of us too. It also meant that my mother and I adopted that neighboring family in tacit agreement, even though they seemed to us as sweet as they were ridiculous and united.

We used their telephone—although I never made or received calls, it was always my mother who ran her communication center from Elvira's house. All this despite the fact that it seemed impossible to us to live among the vulgarity of the crochet, the Swiss cotton tulle, and the clear plastic coverings. After all, we thought, what would we think of our own decorations if we walked into this apartment on the third floor and instead of living there ourselves, we were visiting the home of some distant relatives?

My mother said that books made all the difference, and that I should look out for them whenever I entered someone's home. If they had books, that was another thing.

One time Darío invited me over to his house to study. We had to prepare a project for the science fair at school and he loved my little steam boiler, a toy that worked when you lit the fuse and added alcohol. It would heat up the water in the little bronze boiler and turn it into steam, which would make a tiny wheel turn. Darío was a master of opportunity, with the *porteño* habits and wiles well rusted on. Backed up by his father, who made up a speech explaining how the steam engine worked, which of course had nothing to do with the requirements of the science fair, Darío decided that my little steam boiler would be our project.

And our brash little apprentice wasn't mistaken. Our project was a huge success. It was incredible to see the faces of our teachers and classmates, so fascinated that it seemed they weren't aware of the risk and the fraud of the project. All we had to do was show the steam boiler, and we received an "Outstanding," and Darío let it be known that I should let him keep the toy because he was the one who had figured out how to make use of it, how to turn it into something the entire school considered extraordinary.

But luckily I was able to use my greatest resource, my most effective weapon, one of those talents that comes from nature and can't be learned in any university; to avoid giving him the toy, and also to avoid conflict, I pretended to be stupid, the kid who doesn't quite get it, the dummy. I just gave him a dopey smile with big, empty eyes.

When I had successfully concluded the affair of the steam boiler, through a mix of total misunderstanding and brazen uncertainty, I managed to obtain another "Outstanding," but this time I earned it myself. And it was conferred upon me with mute cheers, olive wreaths, and a twenty-one-gun salute in front of the Sphinx of Giza. I suppose I was unaware at the time, but I could still take on that boastful little tin god and bewilder him with a dose of my Hellenic cynicism.

The first thing I did when I went into Darío's house was scan the horizon for my target: the bookshelves. There weren't any. But in a little shelf unit there was a complete set of twelve books with brilliant white spines and black lettering that said *Encyclopedia of the Second World War.* Each volume had a subtitle as well, in smaller lettering: the Concentration Camps, the Warsaw Ghetto, the Trains to Treblinka.

I wandered over distractedly to look, and I saw that the cover of the first volume was visible, featuring a photo in sepia. It took me a while to comprehend what I saw. It took me even longer to realize that it was impossible for me to fully recognize the forms depicted on the cover that looked like a manual. All I can recall is that in the picture I saw, there were shoes, many shoes. It might have been a mountain of shoes, but I can't quite remember. Or maybe they were unthinkable shoes, shoes I had never seen before. Untellable shoes.

Until my mother and I told her she could come in, Elvira never even put the tip of her slipper in our apartment. When I closed the door, our neighbor let out a few general commentaries about the cleanliness of houses. I suppose she assumed my mother was working on it at the time because she saw the ladder next to the pile of books on the ground. Eventually she said, "Well, you see, I wanted to ask you both something. Well, because you two are on your own, you see, so . . . Well, I thought that, seeing as Christmas is coming, we could spend Christmas Eve together, with Ñatita and my sister, who is coming down from Santo Tomé. I mean the Santo Tomé in Corrientes, not the one in Santa Fe that no one's ever heard of. You see, I asked her to bring some sweet papaya—you can't get it here. She'll probably bring panela and roasted cacao husks, and she's promised for the longest time to bring me a little pair of lapwings for the patio. And I thought we could each make something nice. I can make meatloaf, which we can have hot or cold, or *vitello tonnato*, which are little slices of veal with mayonnaise and pickles, and fruit salad with moscato, which goes so well with Zuppa Inglese, my sponge cake layered with custard."

My mother and I looked at each other, and we were both smiling. I didn't know what half the things Elvira listed even were, and the image of a woman just like her who was coming all the way from Corrientes excited and disturbed me in equal measures.

"What's your sister's name?" I probed.

"Desiré." The word came from her mouth like a huge bunch of gladioli wrapped around many times with a plastic ribbon that was meant to look like satin and finished up in a great bow.

In my mind, I was stuck with the image of a tall, stout lady dressed entirely in pink and who approached along a dirt path with bags full of squawking birds and monkeys who jumped out to steal fruit from her hat, before hiding again and throwing the peels at the birds, and everything would be made of crochet and Swiss cotton tulle.

The smile was enough for my mother to say yes, that it seemed like a wonderful idea, that she didn't like Christmas too much, but that Christmas Eve was a time to spend with your loved ones and how was she going to keep the lapwing birds on the patio without them escaping?

"Ah yes, you have to clip their wings so they can't fly off," said Elvira, dealing with the first of the mysteries in my mind, the pair of birds, the panela, and the cacao husks.

"Maybe it'd be better if she didn't bring the birds," I suggested, imagining birds with purple scars on their sides, sitting on a perch on the cold tiles of the patio, beaks against the wall, surrounded by gray and striped and succulent plants in massive pots.

The plan seemed wonderful to me. For a long time I had known that Santa Claus and Christmas were the biggest lies in the Western world, but having Elvira and her sister and Ñatita come along was the perfect excuse for my mother to celebrate a little, and for me to receive a little present.

"And I can make mash!" I yelled with glee.

"Oh yes, he makes a mean mashed potato, let me tell you," my mother said to Elvira.

"And she can make bangers!" I yelled again, this time hoping to include my mother in a Christmas menu that met her capabilities.

"Wonderful! How lovely to sort it all out. I'll expect you at mine, then?" proposed our neighbor.

And my mother, quick as a flash, made a counteroffer. "Wouldn't you prefer to have it here, and then we can open up the balcony if it's hot? Go on, that way you won't have to clean up."

Elvira's eyes filled with tears, and she ran over to kiss my cheeks and ask me to flutter my eyelashes. She wet my cheeks with her cold saliva, then picked me up and began to dance a waltz with me in her arms and began to sing in her old porcelain doll voice, "Sweet spring, happy spring . . ."

It was a few days until Christmas Eve, and that gave us time to prepare. My mother moved the furniture around and cleaned underneath everything. The next day she returned the furniture to its original geography, but she filled my bedroom with the oldest items and a few ceramic vases. When she saw the air-filled living room, emptied of the old things she had put in my bedroom, she said, "Doesn't this look much better?"

I wanted to tidy up too, so I went to my room and put all the old things and the ceramic vases inside the closet. Then I moved the furniture so I could sweep up underneath. I went to the kitchen to fetch the brush and shovel, and when my mother saw what I was doing, she stopped me. "What are you doing with that? Put it down, you'll make a mess. Why don't you go and play with kids your own age?"

Before I could tell her that the only kids my age around here were the ones in the building, and that I barely knew them and was embarrassed, she said something else. "Do you want to call Darío? In a little while, I'll borrow Elvira's telephone, and we'll invite him over," she proposed as she lit a cigarette, plumes of smoke still rising from another cigarette in the ashtray in the living room.

I remembered my friend Santi, his evil glee and his clenched fists and his hunched shoulders. I remembered the warmth and candor with which he invited me to get to know him. A wave of sweet honesty hit me hard in the chest. Wounded, I returned to my bedroom.

I put the furniture back in its place. Behind me my mother arrived with the brush and shovel, the cigarette in her mouth. "Go and watch your cartoons for a while so I can tidy up," she said while squeezing her right eye shut to stop the smoke getting in. A cylinder of ash, like an extension on a spaceship, broke off suddenly and fell to the Martian surface of worn parquetry in my dominions.

While I was watching television the doorbell rang again and I ran to open the door, while my mother yelled at me again to ask who it was first, and once again, the tips of Elvira's slippers appeared in our doorway. "You have a phone call. It's urgent."

I heard the rasp of the broom falling to the floor, and I saw my mother emerge from my bedroom, cigarette in hand.

"I'm coming!" She ducked into the bathroom, tossing the cigarette into the toilet and, after flushing, left the apartment and shut the door.

After a few moments I followed her, crossing the tiles in

the hallway that separated our apartments, and very quietly entered Elvira's house, standing on the cool, dark parquetry of the landing, which smelled like cellophane candy wrappers. When I edged a little farther in, I didn't realize, but the white light coming from the kitchen reflected off the floor, illuminating one side of my face. Elvira's eyes and the almost white eyes of Ñata caught a glimpse of my serious face. In silence, I tried to hear who my mother was talking to, what she was saying, what tone of voice she was using for this very urgent phone call. I was in full sight of my neighbor and her dog as they sat on the sofa, but my mother's back was turned to me, and she hunched over with the phone in her left hand, pressed to her shoulder, covering the mouthpiece with her right hand so none of the information could escape. While I tried to strain all my senses to put together the jumble of words and sounds coming from my mother's mouth, any little snippet of information, a terrible noise froze the four of us in our tracks. For a second the silence shattered into fragments.

A gust of wind had slammed the door to our apartment shut, and standing there on the parquetry, I came to the realization that our keys were on the other side of the door. Elvira held on to Ñata, and their eyes lowered to the ground. My mother turned around, her face contorted with fury and with one hand over the mouthpiece to stifle her shouting, she looked at me deeply, as if terrified, and without making sound, just moving her lips and fixating on me with her brown pupils, she screamed, "What have you done?"

Then she went back to her urgent phone call and explained that she couldn't keep talking, she had to go. I stood there as if rooted to the spot by the seam of white light that touched my face. My mother hung up and leaned for a moment against the table where the telephone sat, her back still to me. Elvira put Ñata back down on the sofa and looked up at my mother.

"I think your door closed on you," she said timidly, but trying to help. "I'll have to see if I have a copy of your key, otherwise we can try mine. One time I was locked out, and I managed to open the door with the key from downstairs. When keys are old like ours, they can open anything."

My mother turned around. Her face was ashen, and she pulled her hair back and held it at the nape of her neck. She approached me in complete silence, stopped by my side, and put her left arm around my shoulder, pulling me to her. It was a strange embrace, a sideways embrace: strong, sad, silent. I'm not sure if my mother ever embraced in this way again, as if that embrace was an urgent communication, loaded with pieces of information in fragments too diffuse for me to understand at my age that they formed part of a whole that I needed to put together.

What have I done? I thought. *How will we ever get back into our house?*

Elvira strode over until she was in front of us. "Why don't you leave him with me for a while?" she proposed. I realized that my mother had begun to cry in silence because I caught sight of a single tear turned into a prism of light, falling before me as if in slow motion, a rainbow teardrop against the backdrop of a dark room.

My mother nudged me away gently with her flat stomach and Elvira pulled me toward her with her hand.

"I don't know what to do," sobbed my mother discreetly.

"Go on, leave him with me for a while. I'll show him what I'm cooking for tomorrow."

My mother withdrew silently, and Elvira took me into the kitchen, opened the fridge, and showed me half a leg of ham.

"I went all the way to Torgelón, and I bought half because a whole one would be too much. I shared the other half with another lady who also wanted some. To bring it back I had to hire a car service. You can't imagine how much it weighs. I'm going to slice it using the machine, and then I'll put it on the platter, in little rolls, some with a black olive and others with a little maraschino cherry. You know, I don't like bittersweet things, but that's how they do it. And if anyone else doesn't like it, they can just take it out because it's all held together with a toothpick. We'll have that for the appetizer, along with *olivier* salad.

I stopped to look at a little packet of paper sitting next to the ham.

"You want to have a look at this?" Elvira took out the packet, put it on the table, then took out two spoons from the drawer and opened it. Inside the gray wrapping paper was a little jar of *dulce de leche*.

The first spoonful filled me with a surprising joy. I was about to ask Elvira why my mother was crying, but that would be like pushing the spoonfuls of happiness we were sharing up to the precipice of a cliff.

"Come here, Ñatita, come here." Elvira used a silly voice to call the dog. I heard the dog's claws and its first steps on the parquetry, and then she appeared around the corner with a look on her face like Mr. Magoo and wagged her tired tail. Elvira dipped her spoon into the *dulce de leche* and offered it to the dog. Then it seemed like Ñata smiled and came over and licked at the spoon energetically until nothing was left. I watched her from behind, her haunches almost bare, her tail hanging like a dead rat, but her tongue as fierce as a gladiator among a pile of corpses.

I left my spoon to one side and told Elvira I wanted to watch TV. I went to the living room, which was still as dark as night, sat down on the sofa, and fell asleep.

"Helloooooo, who's speaking?" I was woken by the ringing of the telephone and the excessively inquisitive tone of the voice answering, with its exaggeratedly elongated vowels. Ñata sat waiting underneath a chair, a rest stop in her journey around the living room, her blind eyes resting upon me with the perfect silence of a cotton picker waiting to be paid once the boss has blown his whistle. Without my realizing I had taken her place on the sofa—and I'm not sure whether it was because she was good or well-mannered or just toothless—she waited with resignation for the occupation to be over.

Again the call was for my mother, who arrived and made clear signals for Elvira to say that she was not there. Her eyes were red, and her face was still ashen. Elvira picked up the phone again and twice denied my mother was there. In the course of her third denial the communication dropped out. The other person had hung up. They looked at each other.

"How did you get back inside?" I asked. Elvira switched on one of the lamps covered in cotton tulle, and the room turned pink. The phone rang again, and this time it was my mother who ran to answer it, saying, "I won't go, I won't go."

There was a moment of great vitality when the color rushed back to my mother's face and Ñata's whole body tensed, from the tip of her tail through to her head, and her ears shot up straight like two pointy cones, as if she were an English setter that had just caught the scent of a fallen duck, and not an animal of pedigree undone by too much human attention.

I suppose Swiss cotton tulle is a good choice to use a more vibrant palette of colors, because the light from the lamp definitely chased away the shadows for a few moments. My mother hung up, and Elvira looked at her.

"Who was it?" The telephone rang again as she asked the question, and Elvira said to leave it, that they would get tired of calling.

My mother turned to me and suggested we go home and continue the preparations for Christmas Eve, which was the next day. I had never seen her so enthused by Christmas, and I was excited to think that at last the baby Jesus would find in our home a nice place to bring his cow, his donkey, his young mother, his abusive father, his star of Bethlehem, his bizarre Wise Men, and his manger full of straw so that he could get started on the most scandalous vaudeville show in Western history.

"And we have to make some lunch. With so much drama we haven't had anything to eat," said my mother in a tone that showed nothing would sway her intentions. "How would you like some sausages?" Once again she offered the same meal that I would happily eat for every lunch and every dinner for the rest of my life.

"Wait," said Elvira. "Why don't you leave him with me this afternoon? The Titans of the Ring will be at the Riestra Club, and they let me in for free. We'll just take the 44 bus and spend the afternoon there, I'm friends with the girls in the co-op, and we can have a hot dog there." Then she looked at me and said, "What do you think, shall we go?"

The idea of seeing the Titans seemed very strange to me, but taking a bus with Elvira and spending the afternoon far away from our apartment filled me with enthusiasm. I just smiled and my mother accepted, with relief.

"Come on then, let me comb that bird's nest and change your T-shirt."

. . .

A short while later Elvira held me by the hand as we waited at the bus stop. I think she was more nervous than I was because she didn't look at me, but held on tight with a sweaty hand while scanning the horizon for the red and blue 44 bus. She would shift her weight from foot to foot and look out intently, as if she could make the bus materialize through her urgency. She didn't seem calm in the street, as if it were a space where anything could happen, and only the arrival of the hulking twenty-seater would mean we were on our way to friendly territory.

I had never been to the Riestra Club, I had never been to Pompeii, I had never seen the wrestler known as the Mummy, and I had never been out alone with the world's biggest fan of Swiss cotton tulle.

Elvira reminded me of Santi's mom and his sister, and she also made me remember the slap, his mother's shove, the dress covered in orange dust, the shock felt by that woman at the sound of the slap landing on her daughter's cheek. I thought I might come across my friend again, sitting on the bench of wooden slats, in the middle of a bluish mist like I'd never seen anywhere else, waiting for me without knowing it in the botanical gardens, ready for me to tell him all about my trip to see the Titans, like a rascal whose chest trouble settles down with the fresh air of friendship.

During the journey Elvira still wouldn't look at me. We traveled along on a bench for two people—I called dibs on the window seat, and from the aisle seat she strained to keep her eyes on the road, her hands gripping her purse like a pulpit. Eventually, to calm her down, I asked her to sing me a song, and then she left her sentry post, looking at me with a kind face, and sang one of my favorite tangos to me in a low voice, looking me right in the eyes, one that she always sang and that I knew by heart: "Leave me alone, I don't want you to kiss me, because of you I am suffering the most painful torture; leave me alone, I don't want you to touch me, those hands hurt me, they hurt me, and they burn me."

I hated myself for being so good: Elvira's soft voice drifted into ever more lurid warbles that attracted the attention of the other travelers, and she, giving in to her songstress's spirit, never once took her eyes off mine or bothered to lower her voice, rising each time a passenger turned their head to watch. I tried to remain attentive as long as I could, then at one point I turned around quickly to see if something outside the window could be my salvation. But Elvira, a giant squid entrancing her prey, gently tugged at my hands and brought me back to her intimate tango. I hated myself so much for being so submissive and so easily giving in to embarrassment that the only thing I was thankful for was that this scene had not transpired in the botanical gardens, in front of my friend Santi.

Entering the atmosphere of the Riestra was an event in itself. Even outside, before you passed through the doors, you could feel how the air was heavy with the expectation of momentous events, and Elvira began scanning the horizon again for something familiar that would provide her some comfort. She had put on a lot of makeup, and it wasn't Sweet Honesty she was exuding—thank God it wasn't—but her perfume smelled a lot like Siete Brujas.

As soon as we entered the club we began to receive greetings, but Elvira seemed to be in a hurry and didn't want to stop. What

I remember clearly is that, despite a feeling of the county fair in the room, there was something solid in the atmosphere, something palpable that drew you in. A province in the air, an invisible nation, very much alive, noisy and bloody. When we reached the secretary's office, "the girls," as Elvira called them, all stood up straightaway and greeted her, moving toward us like bunny rabbits from a cartoon.

"Look who I brought along, look at these eyelashes," she said, shaking my hand at them, the hand she had never once let go. "All eyes he is, girls, the love of my life."

Elvira strutted about in front of a gaggle of women who looked very much like her, who surrounded me with cackles and lewd winks straight out of the old movies. I can't remember how many times I had to acquiesce to those ladies, each time they asked for more and more, and they seemed so happy when I slowly flitted my eyelashes for them. I was at ease and held court like a sovereign draped in ermines in the middle of a winter of lush trees festooned with tiny twinkling Siberias. I surveyed my dominions, more in command than ever before and with an ecstatic and satisfied harem, the likes of which I would never experience again.

In the midst of so much excitement I realized that Elvira's hand had unwittingly released mine, and I saw the fabric of her dress and the stockings on her legs and her heels slipping away among the women toward the door while she asked the rest of them to look after me, promising to come back straightaway. The girls let out another round of cackles and comments that I couldn't understand, and I began to feel like the character El Mudo from that old Carlos Gardel film, standing on the balcony of a hotel, the skyscrapers of New York in the background, surrounded by the loose beauty and the hair with undyed roots of Peggy, Betty, Julie, and Mary.

"Are you thirsty, honey? Do you want something to drink?" asked one of the girls, and conferred upon me the excitement of a new certainty: I was a honey with the thirst of a legionary in the desert.

A little overwhelmed, but nonetheless unable to let go completely of the sophisticated character that, until that point, I had portrayed so well on the stage, I asked shyly for a Delifrú tomato juice.

Right away I was taught a lesson that I'm not sure I was able to comprehend all at once. The only response I received was the dismissal from those who until now had adored me. New York turned its back on the famous *Morocho del Abasto*, and the secretaries returned to the normality of existing for purposes far more bureaucratic than mine. Something had happened, I realized, just as I heard, "A what? Here we drink yerba mate, or Komari and soda. Do you want a glass, honey?"

Elvira came back after a while with her hair flattened and a noticeable nervousness. Where's the love of my life, she called out, as she entered the secretaries' office, and the girls smiled.

"Come with me and I'll take you to the dressing room, then you can meet all the guys." She took me by the hand, we crossed the hallway, the bocce court, the tiled courtyard with the ring where the Titans would meet, and then off to the side we arrived at a narrow room divided by metal lockers, a window high on the wall and some lamps sitting on a long bench in front of a mirror.

It was difficult to move around in this space, and although there was no door and it was wide open, I knew immediately that we were entering a private space, and that we were allowed in only because Elvira was a friend of the organizers. I didn't want to go in, I didn't want to be there at all. I had never been interested in the Titans and their wrestling matches, and I was scared of those big men in leotards who were putting make up on each other that dripped slowly off the edge of their faces, in the furrows of their wrinkles. They patted my head like so many Saturns wiping their scythes clean on my hair after slicing off the testicles of their father. They put their faces too close to mine, contorting them with false sympathy, and they all sounded like that old actor Pepe Marrone when they called me *cheeee*, drawing out the sound of the *e*. Elvira was excited, and she introduced me to each one of them as they got ready. I didn't know what to say or how to look, or how to act like a little boy finally living a long-held dream.

There was no way these scenes of apparent happiness could compare with those fierce settings where the light was blue and misty, where little boys pull down their pants to show their crusts of eczema, where little girls who are too sure of themselves are burnt at the stake with humiliation by witches.

And my mother couldn't be farther away from this gymnasium, rippling through the surrounding air like an underwater current that comes from the depths of some extraordinary ocean. All of the characters here were determined to make me happy, and they raised their voices to spur each other on in the face of my dismay and my resounding failure to etch a smile on my face. Neither the tenderness I felt at my first solo adventure with Elvira, nor her clear intention to offer me something exclusive, nor even those florid old ladies whom I offended by asking for the bitter cocktail of my sophistication could sway me.

I felt like a pot-bellied monster wearing bloomers with

worn-out elastic in plain view of the whole world. I felt like I had a clown's face painted over my own somber expression with wax crayons.

"He's overwhelmed," said Elvira, excusing me to her half-dressed friends. "That's why he's looking around all scared with eyes like dinner plates."

Deep inside I forced myself to practice speeches of euphoric gratitude, of uncontrollable enthusiasm, I tried to push myself toward a childhood without deceit, without suspicions, but the truth is that I didn't want to be there. I was worried about my mother.

Then it occurred to me to take everything in carefully in case I ever met again with my friend Santi. That made it interesting once more and I took note of everything in silence so I could tell my friend about my adventures in the Riestra Club with the Titans. Perhaps my friend would be enchanted by these characters, perhaps my stories would give him ideas about a possible future, far from the woolen clothes made by his mother, far from the moving target of his sister. Perhaps my chronicle of the Riestra Club would restore him to his rightful place—Santi the marvelous respirator, a superhuman blessed with extraordinary aim, capable of inhaling unimaginable quantities of oxygen and hitting every target with his stones.

After that everything became a film of colors that passed so quickly that everything seemed white, and that dampened my enthusiasm for commentary for my friend with the breathing troubles. Meanwhile Elvira, who was entranced, looked back and forth between the ring and her friends, the big men, and it seemed she didn't know how to behave with me, how to enthuse me. Her body swayed gently from side to side as if each impulse to suggest some way I could become involved was countered by another that made her hesitate and resist any attempt. The most titanic struggle took place inside me: I wanted to be someone else, I didn't want to be there, I didn't want to see the flaccid buttocks of those fallen strongmen. I didn't want to hear any more shouting or loud noises, no more horror, no more reproaches for everything I knew and kept to myself.

I was worried about my mother, about Christmas, about the lady coming from the swamps up north and her bestiary of clipped wings.

When the fights had finished—I suppose the referee was won over by the mixture of sweat and makeup pouring down the faces of the Titans—they started with those speeches where one of the giant men dedicated all the effort of the event to the children's happiness. I suppose we never shared the same observational techniques because in my field study—everything I had seen throughout the spectacle in the ring—the majority of the children bawled at their mothers or organized their own wrestling matches among the seats in the audience.

Then everything began to fade away, and the smiles fell away, while someone began to sweep up and others stacked the long wooden benches. A whisper escaped Elvira's lips; I thought she was going to ask me to sing "*Madre del alma mía.*" One of the girls from the secretaries' office heard and put her arm around Elvira's waist, nodding to me and saying, "Why don't you come back to the office and have a couple of matés before you run off with that cutie pie?"

Elvira took me by the hand, and I felt like Lili's suitcase when she steels herself to take the path of loneliness. Something in the air had changed.

We went to the office, and the girls surrounded us. While one prepared a maté, holding the silver thermos and adding spoonfuls of sugar, others competed for a spot by my side. Suddenly Elvira said that it was best to leave straightaway, we had to wait for the 44 and she didn't want it to get dark on us.

"Won't you sing us a waltz?" asked one of the girls. Elvira smiled, took me by the hand again, and began to say farewell to each of the secretaries. I approved of her decision, and I made up for my prior pretensions of Delifrú by placing a full kiss on each of the rosy cheeks in that office at the Riestra Club.

Something was strange when we got out into the street. Elvira squeezed my hand tighter and quickened her pace. We had to walk a few blocks to the bus stop, and along the avenue silence reigned. Elvira looked behind her while she sped up again, then I wanted to see if something was following us, and she walked faster still. To keep from stumbling I had to concentrate on what was in front of me. When we had almost reached the corner we stopped suddenly; a convoy of cars and huge green trucks turned the corner quickly and occupied the avenue. Elvira crouched down and picked me up in her arms. We were terrified by the proximity of the convoy. The air itself seemed to scratch at our faces. The backs of the trucks were filled with soldiers whose rifles seemed to be at half-mast: they weren't pointing them, but they weren't at rest either. They sped by and looked out at us with serious expressions, their faces unmoving and their eyes frozen just like the sights on their rifles. We were in firing distance of those weapons that multiplied among the soldiers and the trucks. I remembered Santi again, his calm brow and his hunched shoulders, his measured movements that took him to the edge of the pool.

Elvira's body shook gently. Suddenly she began to gasp, trying to hide her trembling. She squeezed me tight and I could hear the air going in and out of her mouth in anxious gasps, and I could smell what was behind her perfume. It was a blue smell, a metallic smell. A smell I knew well, a smell my mother brought home with her after her outings.

Elvira lent us her telephone. I had never smelled that odor on her.

She let out a gasp that in the end she couldn't contain: her legs trembled and she seemed wet, her eyes filled with water and her hair seemed to open up. The convoy finished passing, and, behind them, a few police cars followed. It had seemed like an endless parade.

"They're heading toward the south," said Elvira.

"What's in the south?" I asked, and then straightaway I added, "I want to see my mama."

The world seemed to have been emptied of cars. After the roaring of the green trucks the city blocks were like a model of empty streets and sidewalks, of closed doors.

Elvira began to run with me in her arms, crying silently. Just as we arrived at the bus stop, a 44 pulled up. Elvira began to shout and was nearly struck by the nose of the blue and red bus.

"Hey, what's wrong, ma'am? You look like you've seen the devil himself!" said the bus driver while we were still in the doorway, and some of the passengers burst out laughing.

When we got back, we saw that the door to our house wasn't closed properly. From underneath the door came a few rays of dim light, and from Elvira's apartment there was the incessant ringing of the telephone.

"Luckily Ñatita is deaf," she said as we climbed the stairs to the hallway leading to our apartments.

My mother was a very beautiful young woman, but when we opened the door we found her in a ball on the couch, her face hidden between her knees, the shutters completely closed, without any of the slats left open for air. The dim light came from the noiseless television. My mother didn't seem to hear us, and Elvira hurried over to pull the cord that would open the shutters.

"Don't open them," said my mother in a firm but dispirited voice, shaking her head between the cave of her knees. She was pale.

"Go to your room," she ordered, looking at me for a moment as if trying to smile.

"I'm going to see how Ñatita is doing, and then I'll be back. Do you have anything to eat? The boy must be hungry."

I went to my room and left the door ajar.

I heard my mother, alone in the living room, crying in fits

that just left a deeper silence. I turned on my lamp. The blue light of the television scared me. I heard Elvira return.

"I brought you this. All I ask is that you return the tray and the napkin, they're part of a set you know, and I don't want to lose them." Our neighbor spoke to my mother, and I waited on the edge of my bed for her to come into the room. Elvira came in. On the tray, underneath the napkin, there was a slice of her apple cake with walnuts and icing sugar. Elvira approached me carefully, her eyes wide. What could she be afraid of?

She left the tray on the nightstand next to the lamp; she seemed unable to give it directly to me or to encourage me to eat the cake right then.

"I couldn't do it," whispered my mother to herself.

Elvira turned around and left the room. Meanwhile, the darkness seeping out of the television traced strange images on her legs.

"Do you want me to bring Ñatita over here, so she can keep you company?"

I don't know if she didn't wait for my answer or if she thought she heard me or if she thought there was nothing to say. She walked out of my room and left the door open. In the mirror of the open door I saw the reflection of the television and one end of the sofa where my mother was sitting and where Elvira surely sat also.

The pale blue screen showed indecipherable movements, perhaps because I was seeing the images in reverse or perhaps because I couldn't concentrate. Everything seemed confused, and neither the apple nor the icing sugar held any relevance for me. Everything was a single, poorly illuminated thing.

I don't know if my mother started to mumble again, if I heard her say, "I couldn't do it, I couldn't."

There were letters on the screen, but I saw everything in the mirror, and I couldn't read the words. Now the images were calm. It was a wall with the letters below. I remembered Uncle Rodolfo. I remembered how he would turn serious, stroking his mustache and talking to me. I remember when he told me that I had to study hard, that I had to be curious and that I should never lose my cheer. I remember when he gave me a rectangle of red glass and a notebook, when he showed me how to place the glass in the middle of a page, with a picture on one side and the other blank so I could trace the reflection.

I got up to look for the notebook and the glass. I got out a pencil, and I wrote down with difficulty the letters that the television reflected in the mirror. I knew that there were languages that were written backward—my uncle had shown me. Poor kids, imagine having to learn to write backward and understanding everything in reverse.

There were sixteen letters. Suddenly the light came on in the kitchen, and I heard the sound of water and the kettle, the door of the pantry and the tin with the tea bags, the sound of the teaspoon being placed on the saucer, and the door to the cupboard where we kept the sugar bowl. The fridge door. When we were at home, my mother liked black tea, the water very hot but not boiling, with a big spoonful of sugar and a streak of cold milk.

There were sixteen letters on one side of the notebook, and then I used the red glass.

Elvira was present in the sounds coming from the kitchen as she made the tea, but I couldn't hear her voice or the shuffling of her slippers. Now I heard the water hitting the bottom of the teacup and the torrent that inundated the tea bag and caused the leaves to swell. Now it was the spoonful of sugar, falling into the teacup like a disappearing sand dune. Now the sound of the teaspoon touching the depths of the cup and scraping the sides of the porcelain.

I started copying on the blank page. There were sixteen letters.

Elvira passed through the reflection in the mirror carrying a tray with the steaming cup of tea and set it down on the table. She switched on the lamp next to the sofa, the one my mother used to read her books in the evenings. She turned off the television, and the shadow of our Christmas tree flashed in the reflection of the mirror. Suddenly I had an overwhelming desire for it to be tomorrow, suddenly I had an immense faith that although it was the most scandalous lie in the history of the West, Christmas would fill us with happiness, and we would laugh about Swiss cotton tulle and all the horrible decorations we had made for our little tree.

I finished copying out the last letter. There were sixteen. I placed the piece of glass in the middle of the paper, with my eyes still on the side where I had written the letters, and everything on the other side was stained red.

"Mama, don't worry. Tomorrow is Christmas."

"Yes, my son, tomorrow is Christmas. Now get into bed because it's time to sleep. I'll come and give you a kiss later."

"I'm hungry, Ma."

"Eat the cake Elvira brought you. I know you'll like it. Then I'll bring you a glass of water later."

"Ma, can I read for a while?"

I ate a few mouthfuls of cake and fell asleep. That night I dreamed we were on our balcony, and there was a parade of men walking over to the other side from where we were. I saw the heads of the men marching in silence, and although I couldn't see her, I knew my mother was behind me. It seemed strange to me that we were on the balcony, but I held on to the handrail and tried to stay alert in case the moldings or the ceiling started to fall in. At one point I thought I saw a head of red hair amongthe crowd—everyone marching had dark hair—but I caught sight of a head of red hair just as it turned around to look at me. I began to get upset, and I turned around for a look of reassurance in my mother's eyes, and I saw nothing. I was alone on the balcony. I turned back around, and I began to yell out to those half-closed eyes that had tried to recognize me, to that head of hair that was about to be extinguished. My mouth opened to say "Papa," but the noise of the marching drowned out my shouting. I shouted louder and louder, clinging on to the handrailing of the balcony as bigger and bigger pieces of the ceiling and the walls began to rain down on me. Fixed on that red hair in the crowd, I yelled in silence, clinging to the railing, and although I couldn't see her, my mother grabbed me from behind and pulled me back until I let go and we went back into the house. I yelled louder and louder, and she pulled harder and harder. Meanwhile, the balcony was falling around us in ruins, and I began to hear my own desperate plea: "Mama, let me gooooooo!"

The first thing I did when I woke up that morning was run to the bathroom and look at my hair in the mirror. Then I remembered that it was Christmas Eve. I brushed my teeth and splashed cold water on my face, which was unusual for me, but I wanted to greet this important day with my most respectable rituals. I walked along on tiptoes so as not to wake my mother, and when I reached the kitchen, I found her there standing with her back to me in front of a pile of toast, the last pieces warming in the toaster.

"Look what I've made for you," she said, smiling as she lifted the breadbasket to show me.

Thinly sliced toast was a real treat in our house, and for my mother to greet me with a whole basketful was a sure sign of happiness. This meant we would take a long breakfast together, chatting about places I had never been that she had traveled to once with someone or another, sending back postcards.

Siberia without desolation. Chapultepec without volcanoes. Spain without sons of bitches. The Grand Canyon in Colorado with Navajo princesses and young men with arrows and eagles and red semen. The world was a planet suspended in the fascinated eyes of that beautiful young woman who ran her hands through her hair like a rudder that ignored all distance and led us anywhere on the planet. A breakfast of toast with butter and *dulce de leche* was a seminar on the devotion to curiosity, a training camp in Libya to strengthen the muscles underneath the muscles, the abdominals behind every intention, the aim at a single moving target. It was the pleasure of being alive, a gentle happiness free from the threat of the imminent.

Elvira's voice drew us back in from our wanderings, but it wasn't a tango she was singing, or a waltz. From the hallway we could hear the overblown sounds of a reunion as it made its way up the stairs. It was like the sound of chickens clucking, vowels of happiness and consonants of nostalgia, a broody and scandalous music.

I ran to open the door because I wanted to meet our neighbor's sister, and above all I wanted to see those wingless birds, but my mother held me back before I could even make it out of the kitchen. She motioned for me to be silent with her finger, and with a cheeky smile on her face she led me over to the door so we could listen in to what the sisters were saying. My mother sat down on the ground and leaned back against the door in a single, beautifully choreographed movement. I stood there looking at her and she stretched out an arm to me, inviting me to sit in the hollow between her legs, leaning my back against her chest and placing my head in the space between her neck and her shoulder.

I tried to comfort myself, to play my part perfectly in this choreography, to be pliant and natural and to unwind myself and coil back up into her like the perfect dance partner whose work serves only to showcase the prima donna. Every bone in every joint of my hand, my pelvis, my hips, my ankles, the mobile strength of my feet, and finally my ischium; I'm not sure if I was as good as Nureyev or Astaire but I knew that I was efficient, that

I arrived wholesome and gracious on that promised lap. Sitting in my mother's hollow, embraced by that beautiful young woman's legs, caressed by her hands as soft as peapods, at the mercy of the sweet and slippery aroma of her black hair, so terrifyingly close to the moist skin of her neck, in the unprecedented event of doing something that was not allowed, something that my mother usually would object to: listening in on other people.

I don't think I can recall any of this, but from that moment I do have a single memory of the warmth, the lightness, and the closeness of a living body. I think I understood that I needed to relax for this to happen, and, at the same time, take note of everything and treasure it, so that if the time came, I would be able to tell myself this whole story, in the moments when my doubts were heightened.

I didn't dare open my mouth, but I could barely contain my anxiety to ask her if she felt the same, if my body was palpitating too, if I was emitting heat, if I was just as alive as her. But I didn't dare open my mouth in case my question shortened the duration of that embrace, in case my anxiety to know just how alive she was diminished her. How long did that matchless embrace last, and how did we return to the routine dance of the course of the day?

From the passing of that day I remember the feeling that I didn't quite want to wake up, that I didn't want to change out of the pajamas I was wearing during our embrace, the period when my skin tingled like the aerial view of a sea of city lights in the middle of the night, and my nose wished to slowly and definitively take in all the air around that beautiful young woman who once again opened her legs to receive me.

This was a moment of pure truth, the moment when I was set free from that woman, the moment before the Christmas Eve feast. Santa Claus meant nothing to me, and any fantasy I'd ever held about his beard being red like an Irishman, or a Spaniard or a Viking, all those men who enlisted in history before me slipped away in the trace of his skin in mine. Who, what man, who didn't want to find that imprint on his body, the imprint of a dark-haired woman with noble and pale, bluish skin, so removed from the triviality of the world?

After a compulsory siesta, my mother sent to me wash up, and I had no other option but to pretend I had bathed myself fully. I enveloped myself in the steam of the bathroom, I wet my hair, making sure my whole head soaked through, and I stood like that for a good while so that the steam would open the pores on my face and my ruse would seem credible. I sweated profusely but my essences remained with me: the researchers of the future could run a carbon 14 test on my body, and they would find the incandescent traces of humanity in my skin.

Let it be Christmas, let what must happen *happen*. For hours I felt something in my chest that I couldn't quite understand: a certainty, a calm, a secret happiness I couldn't yet celebrate.

All the wings of the lapwing birds healed, and they thanked their masters for their slavery, like a sacrificial gesture in the face of the clear ineptitude of their owners, like another offering before returning home to tend to their nests in the swamps and to parade about, exaggerating their ferocity so that no predators would ever approach.

Let it be Christmas. Let the Son of Man be born.

. . .

At around seven in the evening, our doorbell began to ring frequently. Elvira was more anxious than anyone about the table setting and doing things right, so she came in and out of the house slowly. When I opened the door the first time she rang, our neighbor hovered in the doorway, asked a casual question, and then left. A few minutes later she came back and rang again, taking a few steps into our apartment, and so on, successively. Each time I opened the door I tried to make out the figure of her sister in the dark apartment opposite, but all I could see was the outline of the sofa covered in parcels and no sign of Ñatita, who had to cede her throne in honor of the recent arrival. What caught my attention was that there weren't any suitcases or overnight bags, what I could see were parcels tied up with rustic string, packages wrapped in old newspaper, and bags made out of old milk cartons and woven into crochet. That was a sign of tradition in Elvira's family; that was the proof that her sister had arrived with her cargo of promises.

In one of those comings and goings by our neighbor, I couldn't hold it in any longer, and before she could get started, I asked her, "What about the birds?"

"What?" said Elvira with surprise.

"I want to see the lapwings."

"Oh, the lapwings. She didn't bring them in the end, but she did bring me some chickens from the countryside for tonight that are just divine. Tell your mother that between the chicken and the veal I prepared yesterday, the salad and some ham with melon, we should be fine." Then she stopped for a moment before adding, "Now what did I come over here to tell you?"

The signs of the most scandalous lie in the history of the West made themselves plain before me, and the changing of the birds seemed sinister. From the promise of a pair of lapwings to a couple of oven-roasted chickens there was a long list of horrors perpetrated by a bloody mob capable of clipping wings, decapitating, gutting, plucking, seasoning, roasting, and crucifying bodies.

"I'll never eat chicken again. I'll never be a Catholic," I promised in silence, swearing before a holy image of myself on an improvised altar I constructed in my head before the revelation of a truth that my mother had always maintained. "Now it's the two of us against the church, Mama," I said again in silence, ending my prophetic psalm.

At that moment Elvira's telephone began to ring. "Ay, I hope they don't wake my sister, she's resting, the poor woman," she exclaimed.

Right away my mother appeared in the kitchen and said to her quickly, "Don't answer—that'd be better, no?"

"No, I was hoping she'd get up soon, so you can meet her."

As soon as she'd said these words, the sister appeared from behind, from the depths of the darkened rooms of Elvira's house. From her size, she seemed like Elvira's mother, or Elvira herself, but with breasts twice as large, her features a little more round, more youthful and flushed. She came out of the apartment, her eyes heavy from deep sleep, adjusting her hair with her hands. When she arrived at our house, Elvira let her in.

"I'd like you to meet my dear neighbors," she said with a mixture of respect and nerves that her sister received with a smile.

"I'm Desiré, Elvira's sister. It's a pleasure," she said, bending down and looking me in the eyes as she held out her hand in the face of my confusion. Once we had shaken hands she bent down a little more and placed a noisy kiss on each of my cheeks.

"I've heard so much about you, young man," she said in a tone that I'd never heard before. She winked and shuffled over to greet my mother. With her she was less ceremonious, more familiar. She wore a flowery dress with a white collar and short sleeves fringed with the same material as the collar. Desiré was a surprise: her cheeks were chubby and rosy, she was curvy, with huge calves and big feet. She had full lips that seemed always to be promising a kiss. Desiré was a surprise: I didn't know why, but compared to all the women I knew, this big country woman seemed extraordinarily beautiful. In each step she made, timid and silent in the worn-out moccasins she wore, she seemed to unfurl something I hadn't seen before. I'm not sure if it was music or the sound of a river rushing over rocks or the rustling of reeds in the wind by the riverbank. I'm not sure if it was her almost-bitter perfume, green and freshly cut, or if it was a strange voice like a half-opened treasure chest inside a water hyacinth filled with bugs. Desiré seemed beautiful, a matron embossed by her geography, the geography of a map I had never seen before. Desiré was big, her skin ripe to bursting. Desiré was fragrant, like a grapefruit warmed by the afternoon sun in a fruit bowl on the kitchen table, and she was standing there quietly among us. But for me, a hidden nation danced behind the fabric of her dress, an entire nation danced there, and no one here noticed.

I had to cover myself, the fabric of my pajama pants did little to hide the pomp and ceremony that Desiré had stirred in my loins. I couldn't remember that ever happening before. Before that giant earthen sculpture, in that living room filled with postcards, before the presence of a beautiful young woman that, for the first time, disturbed me and next to our singing neighbor, all the blood in my body went either to my cheeks or my hard penis, erect and anxious to display itself to this wondrous woman of Christmas.

My penis was exultant, incriminating, erect. And then I was shut up in my bedroom, dying of shame and wishing a thousand deaths on Santa Claus and every single person in the Vatican.

I wanted to dissolve in my mother's embrace, let myself go forever, turn into a dolphin that never had to come back up to the surface, surviving in the depths of the water without needing to breathe. In contrast I wanted to conquer Desiré, to wound her, approach her in a helmet and iron boots up to my knees, I wanted to raze her, destroy everything of her, eat her, melt her down for my own use. How strange.

In any case, it would be best for Santa Claus not to appear, nor any redheaded man. My fanged mouth opened wide, and my penis was like a bloody arrow.

So that was my first Christmas: an orgy that wore itself out before it even began, a feast with three women who watched me, laughed, stroked my hair, and never stopped talking and laughing while I became lost between the staring and the flushed cheeks that those voices pointed out to me every time I stared too long at the woman from Corrientes.

Present time was no less humiliating: My mother's gift was three pairs of underwear wrapped up in little cardboard boxes, along with a bathing suit and a T-shirt. Elvira's gift was another pair of underwear and some socks. Desiré's gift was a jar of sweet papaya, a fruit I had never tasted before, and one I regretted tasting the moment I did.

A short while after opening the presents, my mother let me drink some pineapple fizz, and we ended the night playing charades. I laughed then as well. I laughed a lot. I laughed most from seeing my mother giggling wildly in a way I'd never seen before. Although she lost a bit of her sensuality from shaking so much, my mother looked like a happy woman. And for a good while, I could laugh along as well.

From the summer of wine there remain only a few splotches, as if it were a reel of film that someone yanked fiercely from one end to hurry things along.

I think it was still January when we went on vacation. My mother decided that we had to go camping, and San Antonio de Areco had it all: a river, history, literature, a zoo. We got ourselves a tent, sleeping bags, and someone lent her a Renault 4. I didn't even know she could drive, so I was surprised and excited by the plan. I had never slept in a tent before, and the idea fascinated me. It seemed extremely logical, it was something I'd tried to do before in my own room at nap time. I'd put the mattress on the floor and hang the sheet from wherever I could up high. It seemed like a wonderful idea, although I was startled at the prospect of sleeping so close to my mother. And so we went.

I think I spent the whole trip watching her driving and smoking, looking in the rearview mirror, stopping at gas stations to refuel the car, drinking coffee in little plastic cups, lifting off her glasses and running a hand through her hair, smiling cheekily when she realized I was watching her.

I remember as soon as we arrived we set up the tent by the river, near the bridge and a little dike. The tent was heavy, difficult to assemble, and it smelled damp. It suited us just fine though; it wasn't quite long enough, but it was steady. With some instructions from my mother, I set about digging a trench around the tent in case it rained, so the water would run off and not flood us.

One day we went to the zoo. I remember a leopard lying about like an old drunk on a concrete patio with thistles growing through the cracks, in a tiny cage with just a tiny log and wire mesh. I'll never forget that, what I felt about myself then, although at the time I couldn't quite translate the meaning of the scene. I felt bad knowing that the leopard was there for my eyes too. What I saw was a king without claws, a melting iceberg trapped in a warm current that bore it far away, a solitary caged wonder. How do you turn a force of nature into the embodiment of nothing?

My mother must have noticed something because she took me by the hand and without saying a word led me straight to the exit. We had only just arrived but we left, walking along the sidewalk in silence, beneath garlands of wisteria, chased by heavy gray clouds that blanketed everything.

We arrived at the campground the moment it started raining. First there was a strong odor rising from the earth, and then fell the thickest raindrops I'd ever seen. "Please don't rain," my mother said to herself, thinking I couldn't hear her. We went into the recreational hall, which was a clamoring mass of people playing cards, and we stood there looking out the window, watching the bubbles as the rain fell onto the surface of the river.

"It's going to rain for a long time," said someone near us.

"Please don't rain," repeated my mother to herself. "Please don't rain."

I watched the river rising slowly, the current swelling forcefully and sweeping along branches and plastic bags from farther upstream. I looked at the river and thought of Uncle Rodolfo. The river was approaching, and I knew I couldn't ask anything, nor could I say how I missed the afternoons when he used to come and teach me things about the country or take me out to play soccer.

"Yes, it's going to rain for a long time. A good soak to wash everything away," came the same voice from somewhere nearby.

I think my trench washed away from all the water, and I think it rained inside our tent as well that night. I think we called an end to our vacation earlier than planned because as soon as the sky lightened a little and there was a moment of sunshine, a relentless counterstrike of heavy drops filled the air again. I think it was me who proposed the retreat; it seemed to me that in the face of such a threat we were hopeless and that we would be better off saving our energies and regrouping for another summer. I think my greatest fear was that the rain would soak my mother, would turn her into a teardrop; beautiful women tend to become somber in the face of such dark horizons.

I remember that just as quickly the shadow of the school building reached my shoes on the sidewalk, and I had the impression that the building could crush me. In the preceding days, while getting everything together for the new school year, I found the notebook where I had written the letters from the television that had been reflected by the mirror on the door of my bedroom. The letters I had written down the night I arrived home with Elvira after watching the Titans, when we found my mother balled up in the darkness on the sofa. Those letters I had deciphered and that I planned to write out correctly using the red glass. It was a notebook from the year before, and I didn't need it, but even so I'm not sure why I decided to erase those letters written in black pencil. I opened the notebook and left it on the ground, then I got up to look for the eraser but I also fetched the red glass that was in a drawer. I lay down on the ground, and before I started rubbing the page with the eraser, I put the piece of glass in the middle of the page, exactly where the last letter ended. I didn't have a pencil nearby, but I didn't need it to make out the letters on the blank page, I could read them clearly in the reflection of the red glass: *UNIDAD VIEJO BUENO*, it said.

I erased everything, put the notebook away along with the red glass and the eraser, and made sure I had everything ready for school the next day.

Despite that white reel that someone yanked to speed things up, I clearly remember my happiness at seeing Darío on the first day of classes and how enthusiastically we told one another about the summer we could still feel. I remember that my little trench around the tent became as big as the Zanja de Alsina in the stories I told my friend, the system of trenches dug to protect Buenos Aires from the Mapuches, that the writhing worms I dug up with each spadeful became Indian raiding parties letting out war cries, that the silent river could not be contained and washed over everything, that it came all the way up to the recreation hall and that luckily, the kids playing cards in there had been able to run away just before the silent tide overtook them. And that when my mother was driving she looked like a movie star.

I suppose over the course of the days, autumn accustomed us to normality, and for that reason I remember nothing more until one afternoon at the beginning of June.

I suppose there was no drumroll, like when the tiny trapeze artist launched herself into the air so that the young man with the huge thighs could catch her and steal her away from the void, before the final curtain, all the elephants linked tail to trunk, arms out wide to receive the applause of the public, elephant tail to elephant trunk, and a bouquet of flowers for the young woman, cheers for the young man with thighs like a thoroughbred. And tail then trunk then a rough gray screen. And an abysmal all-seeing eye.

I suppose there was no time for these things, that nobody had time to answer my questions about whether the workers are poor, if Santi is poor, if his mother and his sister are poor. If Uncle Rodolfo has moved away, because it's been so long since he came to visit.

I suppose it was a long time since I'd heard the foghorns on the high seas of the night.

One afternoon Elvira came to pick me up from school, and I was very pleased with the surprise. It wasn't at all usual, and I suppose I must have assumed that an old tango singer always has eyes full of sadness because it didn't seem strange that she didn't speak to me and that she walked next to me in silence, holding my hand gravely along each block on our way home.

When we were arriving at the corner I saw a policeman standing on the sidewalk, and I don't know why but I just took off. Elvira tried to hold me back but I managed to get free and I dashed away, like a leopard tired of lying down before the eyes of his captors.

I knew something was wrong. I knew. I ran madly, gripping my satchel with my notebooks as tightly as I could, and I knew something was wrong. I knew.

When I arrived at the entrance to our building, one of those apartment blocks from the 1950s, modest but elegant, cool in summer, freezing once autumn arrived, I saw that the downstairs door was open. I went in. Elvira was slow to arrive, and

I wanted her never to arrive. I needed to be alone, and I didn't want anyone to take hold of me with the excuse that I was just a child.

From the landing I faced the stairs and began to climb. The door to our apartment was also open, and there was a brilliant white light shining out. A light like I'd never seen before. There was no sound at all, but on the stairs were things, little bits of things. I kept climbing. On one of the last stairs, I ducked down to pick up something I couldn't quite identify. Once I held it in my hand I recognized it—it was a shred torn out from a book.

I arrived at the landing of brilliant white light and faced up to the hollow of the open door. My eyes hurt from all the brightness flowing in through the open shutters, opened up in a way we never did, as if there were no shutters at all but just a huge hole.

Everything was turned upside down. Everything was a mess.

There were no more postcards from extraordinary adventures, no Aztec suns with colored beards, there were no more photos of men and women sent to us by my uncle. There was no boyfriend in a beret with a red star, a beard, and a cigarette.

There was no sofa, no bed. No lamp on the side for afternoons of reading. There were no more centuries of solitude, no more golden branches.

There was no more worn parquetry or stuffed animals on the bookshelves. There was nothing.

My house was destroyed.

I remembered the scrap in my hand, and raised it before my eyes, swimming with light. The pages slipped away by themselves, like dead leaves in that song that says we'll meet again, that you love me and I love you and that we'll be together. Like leaves that spiraled to the ground as the whole world trembled because a very beautiful young woman was returning from somewhere along a path toward me. A woman like I'd never seen before. A dark-haired woman with bluish and noble skin, with hair that is black and lavish as a bullfighter's cape.

I looked up again, and once more I saw white, nebulous light. A light like I'd never seen before. I saw my destroyed house.

I looked down again at the scrap and read the shred that fell apart in my hands.

It was the cover of *The Manipulated Man.* The book dedicated to those too old, too sick, too ugly.

I'll never read again, I thought. *Never.* Elvira arrived and embraced me from behind.

On my desk there's hardly anything but a cup of tea. Leaves from a tin of Earl Grey, when it's possible. Black tea. I like to bring it to my desk steaming and let it cool beside me, the air around me becoming charged from the modest chimney steaming from my cup. I like porcelain cups or old china. I like to buy them on impulse, without searching for them, in local shops. Every time I come across one, I go in and buy the remnants of sumptuous tea sets, old possessions from families who perhaps had to divest themselves of their crockery. Inheritances that went to the state because a little old lady died alone in her house full of cats, the sole survivor of her history, a big house with cobwebs in the door hinges, with a huge jacaranda tree that stains the spring purple, in her house with no gas or electricity, because there's no way to pay the bill.

Sometimes I ask the vendor if he knows where these incomplete sets came from, trying to fulfill my fantasy of gaining all the necessary information to locate the old house and compose a story that, at the very least, has a face that will see me for a moment and remember me.

But every bargain comes from a swindle, and for the vendor it's much better to know nothing at all of the history of the people he buys his treasures from, for a price much lower than it should be.

I like buying these objects, reservoirs of something unknown, vestiges of time crossed with the tiny empires of family and the inevitable advent of obscurity.

I love black tea. Earl Grey from a tin of Asian tea leaves, slightly damp if possible. I want it to appear like an almost solid lake that gradually recovers its lightness as it melds with the air and mixes with the memories of bergamot from English tins.

I like drinking tea in deep sips, when the temperature of the surface and the depths of the teacup become uniform and palatable for the lips.

I love the last mouthful, as rough as a cat's tongue and astringent like nothing else, solid.

I love the stray drop that sits in the belly of the teaspoon, on the saucer, next to the teacup. I love the tiny square of courtesy in the narrow bottom of the cup, in the smaller circumference that holds the tea on the inside and fits perfectly on the outside into the little ridge on the saucer.

I love tea with water crackers, and although sometimes I can't finish it because I can't stand crumbs turned to mush, I can never fully resist, and I break the crackers in half and drop them gently into the tea, taking care to scoop them up quickly so that they maintain their crunchy texture but take on some of the puddles of tea. Earl Grey, if possible.

I began to enjoy the taste of tea as an adult, and I think it required a certain discipline. At first it was more or less an unconscious decision: one day I simply walked into one of those stores and bought a teapot along with the teacups that remained from the set.

I arrived home keen to learn: what blend of which type of tea, what origin, what temperature, how salty the water, how long to infuse. I began to make tea not in secret, but with great discretion. I didn't quite know what I was building, but I couldn't distract myself with questions or justifications. I had never liked tea, my mother drank yerba mate, I drank yerba mate. Who knew what I was doing?

I suppose I needed my own ritual, to build something from the ground up, something that began with me and had no history except for my own. Tea, in a teacup, at a particular moment during my day. A religion, a fetish for my exclusive solitude.

Something of my own.

Maybe I did it blindly, in that moment of blindness when I stumbled across something like a personal truth, like divers who feel their way along in the dark depths of a river. Although this was true, it wasn't without history; I'm never going to have children.

I don't know how I know. I didn't know that I knew it so well, and perhaps the beginning of the tea was the end of that certainty. I exchanged a legacy for my own ritual. I gave up the possibility of a future history, passing on my own blindness to a new body so I would feel better. I gave up the possibility of tying shoelaces on tiny shoes and running to the hospital in the middle of the night, convulsing. I gave up life. For tea.

Fabiana figured it out on one of the afternoons when she saw me at my desk. She came in looking for something and was surprised. She was kind enough to flatter me for a while before bombarding me with questions: The teacup suits you, you look great lifting the cup up and placing it back on the saucer. You look sexy. It makes you look even more silent than you already are.

I turned around to look at her and oblige her with a half smile. I said nothing and changed nothing about myself in that moment, I stayed seated, opposite the few things on my desk, bending over my work, bending over my study. I wasn't doing either of these things. I wasn't doing anything. I was just looking out the window.

Fabiana left the study, hurt. That was our thing, our way of being together. She would bait me and then say something about my silence. I would get mad but never said a word to her. I would have preferred not to get angry, to be a little bit more communicative. I always tried to stay in my mold, not to change or move so that she wouldn't notice my anger, like dry ice that visibly steams but never quite melts.

Is every woman annoyed by the solitude of men?

Fabiana resolves matters by tidying up—she says everything needs to be in its place so she doesn't expend energy on things that can be resolved easily. She always complains about my laziness—she says it terrifies her to see how I can go on living with the lid to the jar of mayonnaise or a knife covered in cheese on the bedroom floor for days on end without moving it.

I can't imagine my life without Fabiana. We have make-up sex and that resolves everything. I never miss her; if we didn't see each other anymore I would think of her as the hot woman she is. I would jerk myself off, remembering the way I'd rub my face across her stomach, opening her legs, firm and pulsing with arousal to breathe in her pussy, rub my nose in it with soft touches, then quickly withdrawing, coming back again and again, faster, with shorter and more precise movements, each time more present than the last. I love fucking her. It drives me crazy to hear her moan, lift her up by the hips, and watch her writhe in the bed when I enter her deeply.

But I don't miss her. I never miss her.

I think Fabiana's main activity is to delouse me, sitting me in her lap to pick at my skull for fleas that she expertly removes, putting them in her mouth and crunching them between her teeth. It's not so bad after all; she likes taking care of me, and that crunching between her teeth gives me a jolt every now and then, keeps me more or less awake.

On my desk there's hardly anything: it's just my desk. It's like a laboratory I've put together to create moments just for myself, a structure designed to induce the idea of work. On that surface I could re-create the frog dissection we did in middle school—a task that was undoubtedly fundamental to my education—going out and catching one of the creatures, putting it in a jar, and bringing it to school for natural sciences class. Who came up with the name for that class, what's so natural about science, what's so natural about this obsession with slicing the critter open just to find out that its insides are the very image of the devil?

First they showed us how to knock it out with chloroform, then how to turn the skin inside out using a scalpel, then stake it out on a slab of Styrofoam so that its inner nature would be fully revealed to us and confess its secrets. Bored, I sat there pressing the frog's heart with the tip of my pen, and I was very surprised to see that the organ would begin beating again with just one touch. The heart is a stupid organ.

The desk sits against the window in my room, where the glass reaches all the way to the floor. During the winter the sun appears in the early morning, warming my feet. I love that. I get up before eight, drink a whole thermos of yerba mate, read a little, trace a possible architecture of the day, listen to music, scribble down stupid ideas, sketch things. A grand moment, a breakfast that takes hours, alone, wrapped in a robe over the top of my pajama shirt, otherwise naked, as I watch people passing by, pulled along by packs of obedient hounds. I swear at the journalists I hear on the radio, laugh like crazy at the journalists on the pirate radio, look at the graffiti on the wall opposite that separates the street from what used to be a warehouse and from the network of rails behind it.

Shortly before nine in the morning, the sun begins to hit my feet directly. It rises up the window and devours me slowly, like an old crocodile. At that moment I take my shoes off, removing them carefully using the tips of my toes, so they land exactly where they just sat, and that way I can rest my feet on the leather.

Two lizards abandoning their shady nest to warm their cold skin.

I live for this moment, and I truly know what it means for morning to break clear, without clouds. A frigate with its sails extended to the sea after a night of fiery and bloody battle. On every sunny day I whisper the "Marcha de San Lorenzo," and only then do I understand the necessity of victory.

Few things make me happy, but the sun on my feet, sitting at my desk in front of the window in my room, is my own private festival, the thing I enjoy the most. And to receive this happiness, all I have to do is place my body there and wait.

On my desk there's hardly anything, but there are things that are piling up. Books that at one point I wanted to read but then get lost right away under another book that won my interest, and so they begin to form mounds of suspended reading.

I began to read again as an adult, partly because of laziness, because I was too lazy to see through my promise of not reading.

After all, that's all there is to do, I told myself. Reading is the only thing you can do.

I like to read anything I can get my hands on, and I like not knowing what my friends are talking about when they talk about literature. I like to read because it is a brutal exercise in unmemory: each sentence strikes out the one before it, inscription after inscription after inscription. Every letter is the same letter, a smudge of blurry alphabet.

Each time I close a book, I forget it. Even the books that can make me feel all the way down to the soles of my feet. Even the book with that poem in it by Emily Dickinson that made me howl as if the winter sun were crawling over my feet, lost in the tides of the high sea of my life, directionless, or with every direction dispelled, like a frog pegged open on a sea of student Styrofoam.

Just the slightest touch from a pen to bring the heart back to life, a slight touch from Dickinson, and the blood flows again, the frigates weigh anchor after the merciless battle. How did that poem go, Dickinson? I have no idea. If I put myself in the air of the morning that I read it, something remains, like the idea of a memory: "I am nobody."

Emily and my heart; a stroke of the pen is enough.

I like to read, and I like to drink tea. Each taste binds itself to the last and becomes definitive; I'm not interested in building anything that depends on the past.

There are very few things on my desk, and luckily every now and again Fabiana comes past and hisses at me. She wakes me up a little; she reminds me of everything I've forgotten, she pushes me up against it, she puts me to work. She encourages me to go and visit Elvira at the nursing home. She insists that I take her freesias or red carnations in the winter. She knows that Elvira likes carnations, that she comes from another time when carnations were considered beautiful and evoked Spain.

Elvira loves to see me. When she sees me arrive, she smiles in her tiny little body and her eyes fill with tears. I kiss her on each cheek and I stroke her face while she pulls out the embroidered handkerchief from her sleeve, wiping her eyes and holding in the weeping that threatens to overcome her.

I give her the flowers, and I give her the pastries she loves that Fabiana orders specially so that all I have to do is stop and pick them up on the way to the nursing home. Afterward it's more or less the same: I hope the afternoon is clear and we can stroll in the little garden, the only place in the entire nursing home that doesn't smell, so Elvira and I can take some tea in the sunshine sitting next to each other on the benches by the blossoming wisteria, holding hands. Elvira takes my hand and puts it on her lap with the incredible softness of her old skin, with the full power of her weak, smooth, loving hands.

We don't speak. I suppose neither of us wants to break out in tears. It can't be easy to grow old, to be a lady who was once a tango singer, to see how the little flowers from the wisteria fall and to wait for the new buds, knowing that there is nothing to do but wait and wonder if you can.

Elvira asks me to sing to her, but I'm a dog, and at the beginning I refuse. Fabiana found the lyrics to a waltz and a little tango song and taught me how to sing them, and so, at some point during the visit, I lean in closer on the bench until our bodies are touching, and then I begin singing, without her even asking. Slowly but surely, as if in another life I had been Floreal Ruiz. "That Ruiz was a chorus singer if ever I saw one," said Elvira one day, and I was stunned by her comment. She likes it when I sing "Old Copper Clock" and pretend to have the mastery of Miguel

Montero. She cheers and laughs to herself, without looking at me, her eyes full of tears.

I have a memory of that nursing home that I cherish, one of those memories I want to maintain, but without the obligation of staying faithful to it, without using it, without pressing play every time I need to know who I am.

That secret is just for me.

I would have been about twenty-five years old, and it had been at least two years since Elvira had been at the nursing home. She was mostly fine; she only tuned out for short, sporadic periods, but she couldn't live by herself anymore. One afternoon I went to visit her, and while we were there, in the little garden out the back, her sister surprised us with a visit. Desiré arrived without notice, and afterward admitted that she wanted to drop in on the nursing home when they weren't expecting her, and she almost didn't recognize me. When Elvira told her who I was, she couldn't help smiling. I saw the very same woman, perhaps a little older, but she had the same impertinent curviness. Those rosy cheeks, her butt as high as the top of a circus tent, and that mouth just waiting to be kissed that opened up to smile at me. Modestly, but without any intent to hide. In any case, the modesty took hold of me, my face flushed, and my dick went hard instantly.

Luckily we sat down and had tea. My eyes went from Desiré to the floor, I couldn't stop looking at her, and whenever I realized I was staring I looked away, too obviously. It was so bad that at one point Elvira and her sister began to giggle too much for my liking. At first it'd made me uncomfortable to be as hard as a post in the middle of a geriatrics' garden that afternoon, sitting there next to Elvira, an old aunt with whom I had to behave myself. But sitting there with the table as a parapet, I could savor the happiness of my cock, even if it hurt a little. I didn't care if anyone else saw me, appearing on the cover of a newspaper as the pervert from the nursing home didn't bother me a bit. I was hornier than ever. The horniest I'd ever been, sitting there completely in love.

That afternoon, when the wisteria was nothing more than a dark stain on the ground, we went back inside and left Elvira in her room to have dinner. The nurse was bringing her food as we entered the room she shared with two other ladies. Elvira paraded me around in front of the old ladies at the nursing home like a flag that filled her with pride. Desiré and I were all she had left of family, and she gloated that none of the other ladies ever received such a handsome visitor. I think they forgave her exaggeration because most of them had children of their own who visited, and she would always sing a tango if asked.

When Desiré and I went out to the street, after kissing Elvira twice on the cheeks, stroking her face, and promising her that I'd be back to visit again soon, without thinking, without being able to do anything else, I took Desiré by the hand and stood next to her. This didn't seem to bother her at all, and she accepted my hand in hers, warm and round.

We began to walk in silence and then at the corner I stopped, kissed her, and whispered, "I want to fuck you, I want to be with you," in her ear. I spoke in a low but desperate voice, unable to let her go, unable to hold back and try something more gentle.

What happened afterward was like a jungle, with a texture I'd never felt before that made me feel like I'd been drugged. Desiré was quite a bit younger than Elvira, but even so, she was still an old woman, a woman who, when I saw her before me, seemed like Helen in retreat, like Malinche, the complete *correntina*.

I couldn't react, and I was powerless to stop myself as well; it was the law of the jungle that overcame me: beasts with lascivious gazes paraded before me, enchanting eyes that opened like fangs. When I walked, all the blood drained to the soles of my feet. I fell into deep holes covered with trapdoors of dead leaves, snakes hissed through forked tongues, nearby waterfalls roared, and the air was heavy with moisture. The corpse of a capybara swollen with maggots, glowworms and butterflies rushing out of caves where vampire bats hung upside down, the unexpected oasis that becomes a trap for the deer, a boa constrictor wrapped around the leg of a cow, sucking milk from its udder, a fledgling frightened by the loneliness of an abandoned nest, an orchid exploding in bloom with no one to see, the delicious perfume that turns from sweet to rancid as the sun reaches the highest branches of the *mburucuyá*.

Being with Desiré was a jungle. We spent the night in each other's arms in a room in the Pacific Hotel. We took naps and started over again and then ended up where we started, in each other's arms. At one point, in the intermittent darkness of the room, she began to speak in a gentle voice, her body stood out from the wall in sequences of green neon light from behind the window.

Desiré told me that I reminded her of a boy who had his first time with her. I never knew if she was telling me she had been a prostitute or if she'd just had an affair with a minor.

"And?" I asked as I began to laugh a little. "How was it?"

With that question I wanted her to see me, just like that, in that intermittent darkness I wanted to appear at last in her eyes.

Desiré sighed, fixed her eyes on me, and answered gently, "I killed him," she said with a proud smile and her guaraní tones, a Chinese rose penetrated by the long beak of an insistent hummingbird.

That morning, extremely early, we left the hotel in the cold of first light. Once we were back on the street, there was nothing between us, nothing. An enormous sadness, perhaps. A sadness in which the monkeys of my first images of Elvira's sister arriving, stealing fruit from her hat, were hidden in the pockets of her dress, exhausted from the dusty trip, a little ashamed.

I invited her to breakfast at the little pizza restaurant underneath the bridge, and we drank coffee in silence while the day broke and everything turned pale. I pulled apart my croissants to find the soft dough inside, and Desiré dipped hers into the coffee. She seemed tired, but little by little, she regained her color.

She couldn't get away fast enough. All she wanted to do was begin her day and forget me.

We never saw each other again. From that morning on and after the long night of the purest love I'd felt since childhood, everything ended. Venturing into the jungle left me more wounded than I could remember.

I didn't know where to go, and I couldn't return home. I was shaking, frightened by the void I had plunged into. I began to walk and tried to feel the soles of my feet, tried to feel like I was truly there, slicing through the air.

In a shop window I caught sight of my reflection, as redheaded as a child, my hair like a wildfire that could set fire to anything, as redheaded for sure as the man who never showed up. Son of a motherfucking bitch, leaving me alone in the world, swapping the chance to tie my shoelaces for something shitty. Son of a million dirty whores, leaving me with nothing to write in the space marked *father.*

I walked along as fragile as the tiny body of the girl in the sequined bodysuit that shot sparks as it caught the light when she let go of the trapeze, with the circus tent in the background, before they packed it up and continued their journey. All the while the young man with the strong thighs, bathed in light like an apparition, stands strong in the darkness, his role essential in the forewarning of the void.

The bodies pile up like so many bones on the side of the road; the circus goes on. Long live the circus.

I began walking toward the nursing home. My heart was a hole opening wider and wider, and all I needed was for Elvira to take me by the hand in silence while I kissed her cheeks and stroked her face, and she took out her embroidered handkerchief to wipe her eyes.

It was far away, but I needed to walk. I realized I would have preferred not to fulfill my little fantasy with the *correntina*, and at last I understood why my mother had tried to save me from Christmas. All that remained from a night in the jungle was sadness. My body bled from the claws of a jaguar, and a fork-tongued poison entered into my bloodstream through my ankle.

I needed the smooth and ancient hand of that body that was there for me then and was here for me now, my watchful neighbor. Elvira could gaze upon me and bring me back to my life of unfulfilled desires.

When I had almost arrived at the nursing home I slowed my pace and saw the shutters of the building opened just slightly, enough to offer a still photo of the film that played inside. Elvira was alone, in her dressing gown, sitting at the table, eating breakfast in silence. Next to her cup of tea was a packet of water crackers. I stood there watching through the crack in the shutters, I could do nothing more. On the saucer, there was a used tea bag, and that image, Elvira's hands, the crackers, the tea bag itself—it brought the whole film rushing forth. I remembered how my mother, when she was at home, used to make her tea very strong, the water almost boiling, with sugar and a streak of cold milk.

Tea wasn't my thing, it was *never* mine. I was just a son, nothing more than a son.

Just then one of the nurses appeared to open the shutters fully, and she came upon me standing there staring.

"What are you doing there?" She began yelling at me but soon the tone of her voice changed when she recognized who I was, and saw that I was standing there crying in silence in the middle of the sidewalk, watching Elvira with her ancient hands, watching her tea ritual.

"Do you want to come in and see your grandmother?" asked the nurse, trying to console me, trying to calm me down. "Do you need a tissue?" she added, and I couldn't even respond.

"Wait here," she said. "I'll get you one."

A minute later she stuck her head out the window and told me to go to the front door, saying that she'd open up and give me some tissues. I had stopped crying. I don't know if I had ever cried before, yet half a minute ago I couldn't even imagine being alive without crying. Now it was over, but I still wanted to be with Elvira.

The nurse displayed a modest friendliness which helped, because I didn't want to have to explain anything, I just needed Elvira to stroke my face in silence, to look at me with her milky eyes, as white as the eyes of the dog she had in her apartment when I was little. When I walked into the dining room she had her back to me, I came up from behind and tried to sing "Flor de lino" in a low voice so that she would recognize me, but it was impossible—my voice was completely gone. I sat down next to her, realizing Elvira could never give me the embrace I needed.

She was so tiny and, while in her eyes she held the flame of a shared experience, a tide of tears always extinguished any deliberate impulse. She was very happy to see me, but she kept eating breakfast as if it were completely normal for me to visit in the morning. A cheeky grin came over her face and then dissolved just as quickly, as if it were too much effort to hold the expression on her face.

We sat in silence.

When she finished her tea, she pushed the teacup in front of her, toward the center of the table. The trembling in her hands made the teaspoon rattle against the saucer. She picked up a piece of cracker from the table and lifted it to her mouth slowly, chewing noiselessly with calm resignation. Luckily we had a few moments of solitude, and I was able to kiss her cheeks, stroke her face, take her soft and gentle hand in mine, put my arm around her, and let her head rest on my shoulder while I kissed her forehead, stroked her back: every little thing I would have liked to feel. I put special effort into everything I wished she could do for me.

When the room began to fill with sounds that presaged the arrival of the other old people, I kissed her cheeks again, leaned in close, and whispered, "Thank you."

In moments like these language needs to be an invention, from absolute nothing it must burst forth like the first word, so her heart can remain in the perpetual glow of my gratitude, the only thing I felt, along with sadness.

I had to hide my face because a tiny sob and a couple of tears had escaped. One from each eye, refracting tiny prisms of light in the air on their journey toward the ground. Weeping is a universal lamp, and tears are like teardrops from a rainbow.

I left Elvira stuffing her handkerchief up her sleeve after

she had finished wiping the tears from her eyes and had stared into mine. In that moment, we said something to each other, we *began* to say something. I started crying again in silence. I thanked her again.

I walked down the hallway to the front door and faced the day. The sun illuminated the same things, but in a different way, it seemed like their possibilities in color were squeezed out, and that when I left the hotel with Desiré, the world was just a pale impression. Now it was the exaltation of its true manifestation.

That morning I knew I would never see Desiré again. And that morning I also knew Elvira was going to die. Knowing that dispelled my sadness. Knowing Elvira would die brought the spring back in my step and returned me to myself. *Elvira is going to die, and I am going to be there to accompany her, to see her, to commend her to earth or fire. What joy.*

On my desk there's hardly anything but my inherited tea. Lately there's some doubt too: who said no, who spoke for me? Did saying no make me think I was embracing him, looking at him, and telling him not to leave? Saying no, in order to have him here with me.

If I don't have children, then he's the only father, and I'll have him forever. Even if it's only the blank silhouette of a passionate and unreliable choice made by my mother, the impression of an impression.

But this red hair is mine also, the scarlet crown of a prince who resists the throne, my own private Elsinore. Am I an impression? Is it the determination of memory that forces me to be an impression?

On my desk there's hardly anything, and each morning a man who appeared from a scattered past sits down in front of it. A leopard in a cage made from redheaded bars, a force of nature reduced to a body of nothing. Does anybody see me?

Hardly anything. I thought it was depression; I thought it was anger. Hardly anything.

One day I got fed up with hearing slogans like "We have the best dead people." One day I got sick of building my own disappearance. I thought it was hardly anything; that I was depressed and that was logical.

I thought it was depression.

Maybe I wanted to get to the surface so that I could breathe that portion of the world's air that belongs to me with my mouth wide open. I had become used to thinking that the beautiful young woman had been weak, that she had been strong. But weak for who? Strong for who? Who thought those things inside me, and how were those thoughts built?

Hardly anything, I thought. A bit of depression. Who didn't feel like a huge ice cream soda? Who didn't want a beautiful young woman to look at him, just one time and with all her difficulty and all her utopia? Who didn't want her to outline that tiny body with her eyes and place it on the Earth?

I lived in fury, drowning from being the perfect son, of participating in the murmuring of that which didn't even need to be said: everything is settled between broken and loyal people. I never heard anything more Catholic than that; I never heard anything more macho or papal. There's no new man returning from among the dead. Not now and not two thousand years ago. There's a beautiful young woman lost forever in horror and a broken man who is drowning and can't distinguish his memories.

I'm a great diver, and I understand things better underwater. There are things that are nearby that seem far away and things that seem two arm strokes away and turn to water the very moment you try to touch them.

Once we went diving from a little boat in the north of Brazil.

We were a small group in frogs' legs, a shoal of neoprene fascinated by the turquoise streaked brilliantly with light, of beautiful colors and expressions, of fauna that seemed undeniably happy. I love diving; in that universe everything seems united. Before taking the plunge, the leader of the group went through common issues to keep in mind: how to regulate pressure, how to come back to the surface safely, how deep to go. But in that environment everything is easy, everything embraces, in just one second you can find everything. I thought of kicking a little, and then I saw it all: the turquoise darkens concentrically and kindly, you don't have to do anything more than let yourself be. It's complete. Breathe? Be a good son, a good grandson.

Fabiana appeared from behind with her commanding presence and distracted me from my liquid Orpheus, we swam around a couple more times before coming up together. Once we were up on deck we spoke with ample enthusiasm about how fantastic that submerged world was and how fascinating it was to suspend yourself before the void. I think we became impassioned enough to sail right through the fascination that Fabiana celebrated in our conversation, but beneath it all she was furious in the way of a woman who has to share her man with a lover.

There's not much mystery to me: the thing is I can't stand it.

Even though my life is little more than a miserable empire of justifications, the thing is I can't stand it. I can't.

I don't want to be the son of a body in the days between kidnapping and the end. I can't stand it, I can't carry it inside me, I can't bear having survived that beautiful young woman and knowing everything that I don't know. I can't be the son of that woman who is smaller than me in the face of the void. I can't stand it. I can't. And I'm not interested in living to tell the tale. I can't. I can't.

. . .

Papa?

(Is this my only private possibility of truth and justice, even though the first has to fold itself into me to release the other?)

I won't pronounce it like a silent psalm to hold me to this complete nothingness. The cult of the absent one. If there's so little there, I want to live among the dead.

I was too sure I'd never hear it.

Now I hide so I can tremble without anyone seeing me. And what if someone says it to me one time, eyes looking up at me, looking up from some tiny little shoes?

What if someone who has returned looks up at me?

On my desk there is hardly anything but a photo. A frame made of strips of lacquered wood with a stand on the back to hold it up. It's a black-and-white photo with the wind blowing in my face and blowing everything away. A photo where the wind whips through the thick black hair of that woman with pale skin and makes the expression on her face difficult to see. We're both in shorts, but I'm also wearing a sweater, a cable-knit sweater that she'd made for me. We're both wearing sandals, she's wearing a white blouse that sticks to her body on one side and on the other seems like it could blow away.

I don't remember who took this photo of us with our Kodak Fiesta camera, standing there calmly in the face of a wild landscape like a wall of low clouds, a tempestuous prophecy of the sky. Standing in the middle of pale grasses, the two of us looking at the camera, on the way to Mar del Plata from Chapadmalal. We were on vacation at the wonderful hotel built by Perón in 1945 for the Metalworkers' Union. A huge mass of towers, like a hospital or a prison, a mass of buildings full of harsh, soviet luxury. Everything was huge and magnificent and austere, and all of us who were there were like comrades in something, as if we were all from the same school. I remember a feeling of shelter, seven possible days of vacation with my mother, seven days among equals.

We had gone out for a stroll, one of those outings where I knew I would have to depend on every last ounce of patience I had, even though my mother made it sound like a safari full of adventures. It was strange to hear how she tried to talk me into an outing that would be torturous and would never present me with zebras, lions, or elephants.

My mother wanted to make me walk, strengthen me somehow, and I suppose to avoid me asking her to take me to the arcade games on a cloudy afternoon.

"You see? That way is Mar del Plata," she said to encourage me on a walk along the barren cliffs. I didn't complain. I stretched my strides as far as I could to catch up to her pace and so she wouldn't scold me, and every now and again I stopped to watch the albatrosses that glided alongside us on the cliffs.

At one point we came across a huge construction site. We had been walking for a long time, and we stumbled upon a concrete staircase in the middle of nowhere, set into the ground and leading down toward the sea.

I never knew exactly what that was, but it seemed to be the same type of construction as the hotel: enormous, sprawling, harsh. There was nothing at all where the staircase began. It was strange, as if the staircase had been built well before the attractions from which people would descend to the beach. But there was something stranger still: there was no beach down there.

Hand in hand, we began to descend the stairs. My mother's tone of voice changed and she must have felt some apprehension because she told me to hold her hand tight, and she leaned in close to go down the wide stairs. All of a sudden it became clear what was so confusing: not only was there no beach, but it was just a cliff. It was a sumptuous staircase leading to the mouth of a precipice, without protection, without any warning of the danger. The staircase ended suddenly, messily, unmade, as if the workmen of this Potemkin had undertaken the construction without knowing about the abyss and had thrown themselves over the edge while the foremen packed up and moved on to another project.

The staircase led to the void. A wide staircase for visitors to reach the sea of the people's summer. No need to bomb the main square in the face of this national architecture for suicidal lemmings.

On my desk there's hardly anything but a photo in a frame. Beyond that frame made from strips of lacquered wood there is a window. Beyond the window are the crowns of the plain trees, the airy crowns of the hardwood trees from Tucumán with its branches like women's legs in black stockings. Further beyond, the wall that separates the street from the large lot where there used to be a wine bottling plant, the warehouses where loads of Cuyo grapes were delivered, the long queue of trucks that were followed by bees, chasing after a home from which they had already been turned away.

Who was that beautiful young woman?

. . .

In those lots you could build things that no longer exist. In those lots you could build a happy cemetery where we choose to lay our memories to rest, an expanse of lawn that stretches all the way from the sea to the mountains where the ideal world they dreamed of still persists.

Beyond the warehouses are the train tracks, a huge space covered in grass and crossed with silver rails on which the trains arrive at the capital, the nexus of worlds. Where a factory stands now, there were once dark cities, the warehouses were once barracks that were captured and emptied and captured again. That wire where socks and shirts sit drying awaits its gallows, waiting for more trucks, the ones that will inject a new mix of concrete to construct shining cities where there was once a blur. Where there were once factories and the Middle Ages, new, ultramodern buildings with views of the river will rise like Transformers.

How powerful the urge to put on a clean shirt.

And what would that woman with noble and bluish skin, so distant from mundane trivialities of the world, think of all this?

What would she think of the lapacho flowers, for example? Would she be enchanted by them if we walked through a park in the last of the evening, the only time of the day that the trees stand calmly?

If I bring my eyes back from the window, the photo frame with the strips of lacquered wood reappears, the harsh photo that displays my face, and hides the expression on my mother's face, her hair as sumptuous as a bullfighter's cape in the wind. The two of us in shorts. Me in the cable-knit sweater she made to shelter me and her in the blouse that holds her back and sets her free.

Should we speak of the scent of white soap, its modest, antifascist, undefeatable cleanness?

Outside the photo there are piles of books that spill over scraps of paper covered with unreadable messages. Things that I wrote down urgently and that I now cannot understand. There is always a cup of tea on my desk, a revolution that didn't last me very long and with time revealed its conservative tradition: black tea, piping hot, a heaped spoonful of sugar, and a streak of fresh, cold milk.

Where could it be, what could have become of that thick, woolen, cable-knit sweater?

It was summer in that photo, but there was so much wind around the cliffs. You can see my whole face, and it seems expressionless, or with an expression that says I knew, without knowing, that I was approaching the unknown peak of her tiny body on the edge of the void.

In my room there is nothing, not even hardly anything. A desk where I sit each morning, opposite the window, a mess of papers, but nothing really. On the walls there are no Aztec suns, no fields of poppies, no tulips in the foreground that hide the image of a little row of Dutch houses. I don't like to travel, every geography ends up seeming like the edge of a cliff for me.

I want a room with walls that say nothing, a room with a window that lets me see a wall where every day something is written over the top of something else that was written the day before. A room where the world outside resounds and all of a sudden makes me head down the street, just as I am, in shorts, my hair in a mess from having recently got out of bed, in flip-flops, running in a lively impulse that I can't contain because I heard laughter, and I went to the window to see, but that wasn't enough. Heading out into the street to breathe in a huge mouthful of air, to approach those girls who laugh like brooding hens. These girls no older than fourteen, the straps falling off their sweaty shoulders. Those girls who laugh as they pull along a massive cart full of cardboard in the street among the cars. Those happy dark-skinned little girls who fight over an ice cream that melts while they laugh, from all the effort of hauling that carriage of cardboard by the wall in the street, the crib of a baby sleeping off its drunken nursing. And me running with my mouth open to breathe in all the air of that laughter, and I don't know what I'm doing, and I don't know what to do, and I call out to them, and I catch up and stop, almost breathless, and I crouch down before looking at them, before I ask them what they're laughing at.

And the girls, surprised, turn around and stop laughing and look at me crouching and heaving, and maybe they're angry because they'll have to start hauling that heavy mass again after I made them stop with my shouting, and they look at each other because they don't know how to react, and then they look at me again. And they roar with laughter full of air. They look at me, and they burst into laughter. And I breathe.

A NOTE ABOUT THE AUTHOR

Julián López is a poet, actor, and director of the literary association Carne Argentina. He lives in Buenos Aires. *A Beautiful Young Woman* is his first novel.

Samuel Rutter is a writer and translator from Melbourne, Australia.